"You're  always ...

With that, Willis .... he door.

"Willis, wait. I'm sorry," Eva called after him.

"You're forgiven. If the boy has trouble in school, let me know and I'll speak to him about it."

"Fair enough." She arched one eyebrow. "I don't have many friends in this new place. I'd hate to lose the first one I made here."

"You haven't lost me. I live just across the road." He nodded in that direction.

A sliver of a smile curved her lips. "I should be able to find my way over if I try hard enough."

"I suspect you can be a very determined woman."

"I have occasionally heard my name associated with that adjective."

"Occasionally?"

"*Frequently* might be closer to the truth." Her grin widened.

After thirty-five years as a nurse, **Patricia Davids** hung up her stethoscope to become a full-time writer. She enjoys spending her free time visiting her grandchildren, doing some long-overdue yard work and traveling to research her story locations. She resides in Wichita, Kansas. Pat always enjoys hearing from her readers. You can visit her online at patriciadavids.com.

Books by Patricia Davids

Love Inspired

North Country Amish

An Amish Wife for Christmas
Shelter from the Storm
The Amish Teacher's Dilemma

The Amish Bachelors

An Amish Noel
His Amish Teacher
Their Pretend Amish Courtship
Amish Christmas Twins
An Unexpected Amish Romance
His New Amish Family

HQN Books

The Amish of Cedar Grove

The Wish
The Hope

Visit the Author Profile page at Harlequin.com for more titles.

The Amish
Teacher's Dilemma

Patricia Davids

LOVE INSPIRED
INSPIRATIONAL ROMANCE

LOVE INSPIRED®
INSPIRATIONAL ROMANCE

Recycling programs
for this product may
not exist in your area.

ISBN-13: 978-1-335-48799-5

The Amish Teacher's Dilemma

Copyright © 2020 by Patricia MacDonald

This edition published by arrangement with Harlequin Books S.A.

For questions and comments about the quality of this book,
please contact us at CustomerService@Harlequin.com.

Love Inspired
22 Adelaide St. West, 40th Floor
Toronto, Ontario M5H 4E3, Canada
www.Harlequin.com

Printed in U.S.A.

Let the word of Christ dwell in you richly in all wisdom; teaching and admonishing one another in psalms and hymns and spiritual songs, singing with grace in your hearts to the Lord.
—*Colossians* 3:16

This book is dedicated to my wonderful
critique partners and friends, Theresa, Deb
and Melissa. Your help is deeply appreciated
but your friendship is beyond price.

Chapter One

"We are in agreement. Eva Coblentz, the position is yours. Do you have any questions for us? Now would be the time to ask them."

Eva gazed at the stern faces of the three Amish church elders sitting across the table from her. She should have a dozen questions, but her mind was oddly blank after hearing the news she had been praying for. The teaching job was hers. She wouldn't have to return home in defeat.

She wanted to pinch herself to make sure she wasn't dreaming. The men were all staring at her expectantly.

She gathered her scattered thoughts. "I've no questions at the moment, Bishop Schultz. I'm grateful for the job."

"Very *goot*, then." He nodded once.

She inclined her head toward the other men. "I would like to thank the school board for giving me the opportunity to teach at New Covenant's first Amish school."

She had the position. One that would support her for many years, God willing. Joy and relief made her giddy. Was she grinning like a fool? She wanted to jump for joy. She lowered her eyes and schooled her features to look modest and professional.

But a tiny grin crept out. She had the job! She could do this.

She glanced up. The bishop gave her a little smile then cleared his throat. "The house and furnishing will be yours to use as you wish."

"Danki." A job and a home. A huge weight lifted from her chest. Her brother Gene was going to be shocked. He had discouraged her wild plan to travel to Maine alone as a foolish whim. Only her younger brother Danny understood her need to go. Gene said she would be back begging for a place to live in a matter of weeks, but she wouldn't.

The bishop gathered his papers together. "I think we can adjourn, brothers."

The meeting was being held in her future classroom. The building itself was so new it still smelled of cut pine boards, varnish and drying paint. Dust motes drifted lazily in the beams of light streaming through the south-facing windows that lined the room. The wide plank floor didn't show a single scuff mark, and the blackboard's pristine condition begged her to scrawl her name across it with chalk. It was a wonderful place to begin her teaching career.

"You do understand that this is a trial assignment," the man seated to the left of the bishop said. She struggled to recall his name. Was he Samuel Yoder or Leroy Lapp? The two had been introduced to her as ministers who shared the duties of overseeing the Amish congregation along with the bishop, but she had been so nervous their names didn't stick with their faces. They were men in their fifties or sixties with long gray beards, salt-and-pepper hair and weathered faces.

"I do understand that my contract will be on a month-by-month basis until I complete a full school year." She had the job, but could she keep it? She had never taught before. She wasn't sure what would be expected of her. Her school days were far behind her. What if she wasn't any good at teaching? What if the children didn't like her?

The man beside the bishop sat back and crossed his arms over his chest. "I have taken the liberty of writing out a curriculum." He pushed a thick folder across the table to her. "We expect modest behavior at all times. You must be an example to our *kinder*."

"Of course." So no jumping for joy. She had the feeling her actions would be watched closely by this man.

"Not everyone is suited to life in northern Maine. Our winters are harsh," the same man said, giving her a stern look.

She decided he was Samuel Yoder, the newly elected school board president. Well, it got mighty cold in Arthur, Illinois, too, and that had never kept her from her duties.

She lifted her chin slightly, not wanting to appear overly bold or prideful as she had been accused of being in the past. "I plan to remain in New Covenant for many years. I'm not one who gives in to adversity easily. I rely on *Gott* for strength and He has not forsaken me."

"That is as it should be. Isn't that so, Brother Samuel?" Bishop Schultz tried again not to grin, but a corner of his mouth tipped up. She liked him a lot.

Samuel Yoder's frown deepened. The man to his right grinned widely. He had to be Leroy Lapp. "You may count on my wife and me for any assistance getting settled in here."

"*Danki*." Eva started to relax for the first time during her interview. A loud banging started outside the windows. It sounded like someone hammering on metal.

"*Das haus* is acceptable?" Leroy raised his voice to be heard over the racket.

"*Ja*, it's a fine house." It was the perfect size for her. A small kitchen, a sitting room with wide windows, a bathroom with modern plumbing and two bedrooms. In the backyard was space for a garden and a large blackberry bush loaded with fruit. She would have a home all to herself. Would it feel lonely? She could always get a cat.

Samuel Yoder leaned toward her. "Our children have attended the local public school up until now. Some will find the change to a one-room schoolhouse difficult. I hope you can handle the situation."

Was he trying to scare her away? She looked down. "I will pray for guidance."

"We'll leave you to inspect your new school." The bishop rose and the other men did likewise.

Eva realized she had forgotten one important thing. "Bishop Schultz, could some bookshelves be added to this classroom?"

"I don't see why not. How big and where do you want them?"

She looked around the room and settled on the perfect place behind her desk. She crossed the room. "Here. About six feet long and three shelves high. I want the smallest child to be able to reach them all."

"It will take a lot of books to fill that much space." Samuel's dour expression showed his disapproval. "We don't have the budget to buy so many."

She grinned at him. "Oh, you don't have to buy them. I already have them. My brother will ship them here for me." A job, a house and with the arrival of her beloved books she would have everything she needed to make her happy.

The men exchanged glances, shrugged and filed out after lifting their black hats from a row of pegs near the door. The clanging outside continued.

Her new school.

Eva savored the words. She had spent the last of her savings to get here, and here she would stay no matter what her brother or Samuel Yoder thought. She got to her feet and turned in a slow circle with her arms held wide. This was her new life. Her new career. Her way to serve the Lord in the newly formed Amish settlement of New Covenant, Maine.

At thirty years of age she would no longer be dependent on her older brother to provide for her. She could make her own decisions now. From the time she was fifteen she had been living off the charity of her brother Gene. Charity he gave grudgingly. She'd kept house and cared for their elderly grandparents who lived in the *daadihaus*, or grandfather's house, next to the main home, tasks Gene's wife, Corrine, claimed she couldn't do because of her poor health. She had all she could manage taking care of her three boys.

It wasn't that Eva had been treated badly. She hadn't been. Mostly she had been ignored. Like the extra cots Gene and Corrine kept for guests. Never thought about until they were needed. She hadn't minded. It gave her more time to read. Books took her everywhere and anywhere. Each evening she would read to her grandparents who had both suffered from failing eyesight. Mostly she read the Bible and the newspaper to them but after her grandfather took himself off to bed Eva would get out one of the novels her grandmother enjoyed as much as she did. Eva treasured the memory of those evenings.

Rather than risk losing Eva to marriage, her brother Gene had steered away every would-be suitor except one persistent fellow. Eva had quickly learned she couldn't talk to a man who didn't love books as she did. She wasn't disappointed when he stopped seeing her.

"Marriage isn't for everyone," her grandmother had told her. "*Gott* must have other plans for you. He will show you in due time."

When her grandparents had gone to their rest within a month of each other, Eva had been at a loss to fill the void in her life until she saw a newspaper ad for an Amish schoolteacher in Maine. Somehow, she knew it was meant for her. God was showing her a new path. She'd never taught school, but Amish schoolteachers received no formal training. She would learn right along with her students. It had taken all the courage she could muster to answer that ad and to tell her family she was leaving.

Clang, clang, clang.

The hammering outside grew louder. She scowled at the open door. Hopefully, she wouldn't have to compete with this much noise when she was trying to teach. She moved to the window to locate the source of the clatter. Across the road she saw a man pounding on an ancient-looking piece of machinery with steel wheels and a scoop-like nose on the front end.

The man was Amish by his dress, not one of the *Englisch* neighbors that vastly outnumbered the Amish in their new community. He wore a straw hat and a collarless blue shirt with the sleeves rolled up, revealing muscular, tan forearms. He wielded the heavy hammer like it weighed next to nothing. His broad shoulder strained the fabric of his shirt.

She saw the school board members get into their buggies and drive off. They waved but didn't stop to speak to the young man.

When he had the sheet of metal shaped to fit the front of the machine, he stood back to assess his work. Eva couldn't see any imperfections, but he clearly did. He knelt and hammered on the shovel-like nose three more times. Satisfied, he gathered up his tools and started in her direction.

She stepped back from the window. Was he coming to the school? Why? Had he noticed her gawking? Perhaps he only wanted to welcome the new teacher although his lack of a beard said he wasn't married.

Maybe that was it. Amish teachers were single women. Perhaps he wanted to meet the new unmarried woman in the community. The sooner everyone understood she wasn't husband-shopping, the happier she would be.

She glanced around the room. Should she meet him by the door? That seemed too eager. Her eyes settled on the large desk at the front of the classroom. She should look as if she was ready for the school year to start. A professional attitude would put off any suggestion that she was interested in meeting single men.

Eva hurried to the desk, pulled out the chair and sat down as the outside door opened. The chair tipped over backward, sending her flailing. Her head hit the wall with a painful thud as she slid to the floor. Stunned, she slowly opened her eyes to see the man leaning over the desk. "I'm fine. I'm okay," she said, wondering if she spoke the truth.

He had the most beautiful gray eyes she'd ever beheld. They were rimmed with thick, dark lashes in stark contrast to the mop of curly, dark red hair springing out from beneath his straw hat. Tiny sparks of light whirled around him. "You need a haircut."

Had she said that out loud? She squeezed her eyes shut. She couldn't see him, but the stars were still floating behind her closed eyelids.

"I've been meaning to fix that chair. Just haven't gotten around to it yet. A haircut is at the bottom of my list of stuff to get done." His voice was smooth, husky, low and attractive. She kept her eyes shut, hoping he would speak again.

"Are you all right? You can't be comfortable like that."

At the hint of amusement in his voice Eva's eyes popped open. She was lying on her back with her feet still hanging over the front of the chair. "I'm not comfortable. Would you kindly help me up?" Unless she ignobly rolled one way or the other out of the chair, she wasn't going anywhere. The wooden arms had her boxed in.

He grabbed the back of the chair, dragged her out from behind the desk and sat her upright with one arm as if she weighed nothing at all. She looked at the long scratches the process left on the floor. It wasn't pristine anymore.

"I'm Willis Gingrich. Local blacksmith." He squatted beside her and grasped her wrist with one hand while easily holding her chair upright. "Can you tell me your name?" It took her a few seconds to realize he was checking her pulse.

The warmth and strength of his hand on her skin sent a sizzle of awareness along her nerve endings. "I'm Eva Coblentz. I am the new teacher and I'm fine now." She pulled away from him.

Willis let go of her arm. Her pulse was strong if a bit fast. She didn't seem to have suffered any serious damage.

The new teacher was a slender woman wearing a gray dress with a white apron over it. She had eyes the color of green willow leaves in the early spring. They regarded him steadily as if she saw more than his grubby face or his soot- and sweat-stained clothes. Her direct gaze was oddly discomfiting. "I suggest we find you a more stable place to sit, Eva Coblentz. Can you walk?"

"Since I was eight months old. Of course I can walk."

The color was coming back into her face. Her snippy remark proved her wits weren't addled even if there was a slight tremor in her voice. She stood, took a deep breath and headed to a nearby bench along the wall, rubbing the side of her head as she walked. "Is this one safe or are there other surprises in store for me?"

She had some spunk. He liked that. "Want me to try it first?" He sat, bounced up and down a couple of times and stood. "Feels okay to me."

She sank onto the bench with a sigh and pressed one hand to the side of her head. "I have collected quite a goose egg."

He frowned. "Seriously? I thought your hair would have cushioned the blow." Amish women her age had hip-length hair folded up inside their *kapps*.

"I must have turned my head to the side. It's behind my ear."

He had been too quick to laugh off her fall as a minor incident. He needed to assess her injury. He held out his hand. "May I?"

She nodded and began pulling out the hairpins that held her heavily starched white *kapp* in place. Her neatly pinned honey-brown hair remained in a large, tight bun.

He gently felt the area she indicated. She did have a good-size goose egg behind her ear. "Is your vision blurry? Do you feel dizzy?"

"*Nee.* I feel foolish. Does that mean anything?"

He grinned at her. "Only that you're human. Sit still. I'll get some ice to put on that knot. I just live across the road."

"I don't think that will be necessary."

He had spent weeks learning first-aid skills before moving his brothers and sister from Maryland to the far north of Maine where medical help might be long in coming. This was the first chance he'd had to use the knowledge he'd learned from a retired fireman turned potato farmer who lived in the next town.

"Ordinarily, I take a woman at her word, but this time I have to disagree. Sit still. I'll be back in a few minutes and you will stay right here. Understood?"

"I will stay," she repeated, closed her eyes and leaned her head back against the wall. Her color was a little pale. Was she really okay?

Something about her prompt agreement troubled him. He was torn between the need to get the ice and a reluctance to leave her alone.

She opened one eye to peek at him. "I thought you were going to get ice?"

"I'm waiting to see if you plan to obey my orders or if you'll take off as soon as I'm out of sight."

Both her eyes opened wide and then narrowed in speculation. "You must have sisters."

"Just one. She doesn't like to do as she is told, either."

"Very well. I promise to stay here until you return."

"That is exactly what I wanted to hear."

Willis hurried out the door and down the school steps. His house was only about fifty yards across the way. He barged into his own kitchen, startling his little six-year-old sister Maddie, who was coloring at the kitchen table.

"Willis, you scared us."

Maddie was the only one in the kitchen. He figured the *us* referred to her imaginary friend. "I'm sorry. I didn't mean to frighten you."

"Bubble says that's okay. She wasn't really scared. Do you like her picture?" Maddie held up a sheet of white paper.

"It's a blank page, Maddie."

His half sister and her two brothers had only been with Willis for a few weeks. He still wasn't used to sharing a home with them, let alone with Maddie's imaginary friend who required a place at the table and was always being stepped on or sat on by someone. Had he made a mistake by moving the children so far from everything they had known? He thought living with a family member would be best after losing their parents, but what if he was wrong?

It wouldn't be the first time. Normally, his mistakes didn't affect anyone but himself. Now there were others who might be hurt by his failures. The lingering fear that he couldn't properly care for his siblings often kept him awake at night. He tried to put his trust in the Lord, but he wasn't good at giving up control.

He grabbed a plastic bag from the box in a drawer beside the propane-powered refrigerator and then pulled the ice tray out of the freezer. He began emptying the cubes into the bag.

"Willis, you hurt Bubble's feelings. Tell her you like her picture."

A knock at the door stopped him before he got into another discussion with his sister about the existence of Bubble. He opened the door and saw Craig Johnson, the farmer he had promised the potato digger would be ready for today. The man's red pickup truck and a black metal trailer were sitting on the road.

"*Goot* morning, Mr. Johnson. I'm sorry but I'm not quite done with it."

"I need it now. My farm auction starts at two o'clock and I won't get any money for a broken digger that's still at your shop. You're new here and I took a chance on you instead of using a machine shop in Presque Isle. I won't pay for something that's not fixed."

"I understand." Willis couldn't afford to lose business if an unsatisfied customer started telling his friends how unreliable the new Amish blacksmith was. He could only put out one fire at a time. He turned to his sister. "Maddie, where are Otto and Harley?"

"I don't know." She held her hand to the side of her mouth and whispered into the empty air. She turned back to him and shrugged. "Bubble says she doesn't know."

Neither of his brothers were turning out to be much help. He held out the bag of ice. "Take this and a kitchen towel up to the school and give it to the new teacher."

Maddie's face brightened. "My teacher is here?"

"*Ja*, and she got a bump on her head so hurry. I'll be there soon."

Maddie got down from the chair, pulled out the one next to hers and helped her invisible friend out of it. "Let's go meet our teacher."

She took the towel and ice bag and rushed out the door. Willis led Mr. Johnson to the potato digger he had been working on. "Once I get the bolts in and check that it is level, I will help you load it."

"Okay, but make it snappy. I don't have all day."

Willis watched his sister long enough to make sure Maddie crossed the road safely and went into the school. He would have to see about the new teacher once he was done here. He hoped Maddie wouldn't tell Eva Coblentz about her imaginary friend or what a poor job her brother was doing at raising her. He prayed his little sister would be too shy to say a single word, but he knew he was going to regret sending her alone.

Chapter Two

Eva opened her eyes when she heard someone enter the schoolhouse. It wasn't the man she had been expecting. It was a little Amish girl about six or seven years old wearing a purple dress with a black apron and a black *kapp* on her bright blond hair. The child stopped inside the door and stared at her.

Eva smiled. "Hello."

"Are you the new teacher?"

"I am. Who are you?"

"I'm Maddie. This is my friend Bubble." The child gestured to one side.

Eva didn't see anyone. "Bubble is very thin."

Maddie looked up and down. "That's because my brother Willis is a terrible cook. Mostly he makes dry scrambled eggs and oatmeal. Bubble hates oatmeal."

"I'm sorry to hear that," Eva said, smothering a laugh. What a charming child she was.

Maddie walked forward with a bag of ice cubes and a white kitchen towel. "Willis said to bring this to you."

Eva took the plastic bag, wrapped the kitchen towel

around it and applied it to the side of her head. "*Danki*. What happened to your brother?"

"Grumpy old Mr. Johnson came and said he wouldn't pay Willis because his potato digger wasn't fixed so my brother had to finish the job. He's always working. He's sorry he couldn't come back and take care of you."

"It's only a minor bump. He shouldn't worry about me."

"Can I ask you about school?"

Eva nodded and winced at the pain in the side of her head. It dawned on her that her students weren't some vague group of well-behaved children. They were going to be real kids like Maddie with questions Eva might not have the answers for; then what? Here was her first test. "Ask me anything you want."

"Can my friend Bubble sit beside me?"

Eva pondered the question. What would the school board say if she asked for a desk for an imaginary child? She smiled at the thought. "What grade will you be in?"

"The first grade. We've never been to school before, but my brothers Otto and Harley went to school back home before *Mamm* and *Daed* went to heaven."

A wave of pity for the little girl swept through Eva. "I'm sorry. That must have been a very sad time for you and your brothers."

Maddie sat beside Eva on the bench and stared at the floor. "It was. Bubble cried a lot, but she was happier when Willis said we could come and live with him."

"I'm glad she is happier. And did you cry a lot?"

"Not too much. Our old bishop said it was *Gott*'s plan for them and not to be sad."

"It's okay to be sad. *Gott* understands that we miss the ones we love."

"He does?"

Eva nodded. "The Lord knows everything in our heart and he understand our grief."

Maddie put her arm around her imaginary friend. "Did you hear that, Bubble? It's okay if we cry. Not right now. Maybe later."

Eva slipped her arm around Maddie. "If we have enough desks for all the students Bubble can sit beside you. Otherwise, she can stay here on this bench during school hours. Does that sound acceptable?"

"She says it is."

What an adorable child. "How long have you lived with Willis?"

"I don't know. A lot of days."

Days, not months or years so her grief was recent. "Were you here in the winter when it snowed?"

"Nope. The snow was mostly gone when we came. Willis says we will see a lot of snow before Christmas. Maybe even before Thanksgiving. It can snow up to the roof sometimes. I like the snow, don't you? I like to catch snowflakes on my tongue."

"I do like the snow." Eva wasn't so sure about snow that was roof high. She would have to invest in a good snow shovel.

"Otto says he hates school. I won't hate school. I think it will be wonderful."

"Maybe Otto won't hate it if I'm his teacher." Or maybe he would. How would she know if she was doing an adequate job or not?

"Will you tell Otto he's stupid if he gets something wrong?"

"Oh, *nee*. That wouldn't be nice."

"Otto's last teacher told him he was stupid. *Daed* and *Mamm* were mighty upset."

Eva filed that piece of information away. It sounded as if Otto's former teacher wasn't patient or kind, but it was possible Maddie had misunderstood. "What does Harley think of school?"

"He says it's okay as long as he gets to play baseball."

"I'm sure we will play lots of ball." That was something she hadn't done since she was fourteen. Even then she wasn't good at it. She'd spent most of her recesses reading.

"My brothers don't help Willis much. He works and works all the time. He never has time to put shoes on my pony so I can go riding. Otto is always mad that he had to leave his friends in Ohio, and Harley disappears into the woods for hours without telling me where he is going. Bubble gets mighty put out with them sometimes." Maddie gave a long-suffering sigh.

"I can see why." Eva was tempted to laugh but managed to keep a straight face.

"You do?" Maddie smiled brightly.

"Absolutely. Bubble is very perceptive for someone so young."

"I don't know what that means. Bubble says Willis needs a wife to help him."

Eva laughed. "Bubble may be right. Especially if Willis is a bad cook."

The outside door opened and Willis came in. Maddie jumped off the bench. "I have to go." She darted past her brother and ran outside.

He shook his head and crossed the room to where Eva was sitting. "How's the bump?"

"Much better. *Danki* for the ice." She handed the bag and towel to him. "Your little sister is delightful."

His expression grew wary. "She is an unusual kid."

Eva chuckled as she got to her feet. "She is that. I met Bubble and I enjoyed talking to her. She's a fountain of information."

His eyes narrowed. "About what?"

"Oh, everything. I really must be going. I have a lot to do before school starts next month. Goodbye." She pinned her *kapp* to her hair as she headed for the door.

"I'll get that chair fixed for you," he called after her.

Eva went down the steps and chuckled all the way to her new house a few hundred feet south of the school. Poor Willis Gingrich had his hands full with his siblings if Maddie was to be believed. She glanced over her shoulder and saw Willis standing on the steps of the school, watching her. An odd little rush of happiness made her smile. She raised a hand and waved but he was already striding toward his workshop and didn't wave back.

She went into her new house that had been sparsely furnished by the school board and church members. Eva had arrived in New Covenant by bus two days ago. Bishop Schultz and his wife had graciously allowed Eva to stay in the teacher's home until after her interview. Now she wouldn't have to repack her things. She was home.

At a small cherrywood desk she pulled out a sheet of paper and sat down to write to her brother. She tapped the pen against her teeth as she decided what to say.

Giggling, she dictated to herself as she wrote. "Dearest Gene. I got the job. Send my books. Your loving sister, Eva."

* * *

Willis thought he had enough time to fix the new teacher's chair, put four shoes on Jesse Crump's buggy horse and get supper on the table by six o'clock. It was seven-thirty by the time he came in to find his family gathered around the kitchen table with a scowl on every face. Thankfully, he couldn't see Bubble but he was sure she was scowling, too.

"I know I'm late. One of Jesse's horses had a problem hoof and I had to make special shoes for him. I'll fix us something to eat right away."

He went to the refrigerator and opened the door. There wasn't much to see. "I meant to set some hamburger out of the freezer to thaw this morning but forgot to do it."

"You should leave yourself a note," Harley said. He was paging through a magazine about horses. He was always reading. Willis fought down the stab of envy.

If Willis could write a note, then he'd be able to read one. He couldn't do either. The most he could manage was to write his name. No one in New Covenant knew his shameful secret. Children as young as Maddie learned to read every day but he couldn't. No matter how hard he'd tried. There was something wrong with him.

He hid his deficiency from everyone although it wasn't easy. He'd been made a laughingstock by the one person he'd confided in years ago. He'd never been able to trust another person with his secret. The bitter memory wormed its way to the front of his mind.

He'd been twenty at the time and hopelessly in love with a non-Amish girl. She was the only person he had told that he couldn't read. He hadn't wanted to keep secrets from her. She claimed to love him, too. He had trusted her.

Later, when they were out with a bunch of her friends, she told everyone. They all laughed. He laughed, too, and pretended it didn't matter but the hurt and shame had gone bone deep. He didn't think anything could hurt worse than Dalene's betrayal, but he'd been wrong. She and her friends had much more humiliation in store for him.

He pushed those memories back into the dark corner of his mind where they belonged. He had to find something to feed the children gathered at his table. "I guess I can scramble us some eggs."

"Again?" Otto wrinkled his nose.

"Bubble says to be thankful we have chickens." Maddie beamed a bright smile at Otto.

"Bubble can't say anything because she isn't real, stupid." Otto pushed his plate away.

Willis rounded on him. "Never call your sister or anyone else *stupid*, Otto. You know better than that. Apologize or go to bed without supper."

"Sorry," Otto murmured. He didn't sound apologetic.

A knock at the door stopped Willis from continuing the conversation. Who needed a blacksmith at this hour? He pulled open the door and took a step back. Eva Coblentz stood on his porch with a large basket over her arm.

She flashed a nervous grin. "I'm used to cooking for more than just myself and I made too much tonight. I thought perhaps you could make use of it for lunch tomorrow. It's only chicken and dumplings."

Willis was speechless. Maddie came to stand beside him. "Teacher, how nice to see you."

Eva smiled at Maddie. "It's nice to see you again, too. How is Bubble?"

Maddie stuck her tongue out at Otto. "She's fine but kinda hungry. We haven't had our supper yet. Willis had to give Jesse Crump special shoes so he was going to make scrambled eggs again, but Otto isn't thankful for our chickens."

Eva blinked her lovely green eyes. "I see."

"Do you?" Willis couldn't help smiling at her perplexed expression. "Then you're ahead of me most of the time."

Harley came to the door. "Let me help you with that." He took the basket from her and carried it to the table. He began setting out the contents.

Otto pulled his plate back in front of him. "That smells great."

Harley dished up his own and then passed the plastic bowls along. Willis thought his siblings were acting like starving animals. He could hardly blame them. He was going to have to learn to cook for more than himself. Normally, he didn't care what he ate or when he ate it. That had changed when the children arrived, and change was something he didn't handle well.

Eva folded her arms across her middle. "I will be going so you can enjoy your meal in peace. Have a wonderful night, everyone."

He didn't want her to go. He stepped out onto the porch and closed the door from the prying eyes of his family. "How's your head?"

She touched it gingerly. "Better."

"I fixed the chair. You won't have to worry about tipping over again."

"I appreciate that." She turned to go.

"The school board hired me to supply and install the hardware in the new building. I'll get the rest of the coat hooks, cabinets and drawer pulls installed tomorrow. Have you had your supper? You are welcome to join us."

"I have eaten. *Danki.* Don't forget to feed Bubble. She's much too thin."

Willis raked a hand through his hair. "I don't know why Maddie makes things up."

She gave him a soft, kind smile. "Don't worry about it. A lot of children have imaginary friends."

"Really?" He wanted to believe her. When she smiled he forgot his worries and his ignorance.

"Absolutely. She will outgrow her invisible friend someday soon. Until then, enjoy her imagination."

"I reckon you have seen a lot of things like this in your teaching career." It made him feel better to know Maddie wasn't the only child who had a pretend companion.

"This will be my first year as a teacher. I was actually surprised that the position didn't go to someone with more experience. Perhaps my enthusiasm won the school board over."

"I think you were the only applicant."

She laughed and clasped a hand over her heart. "You have returned my ego to its normal size. How can I ever thank you?"

He smiled along with her. "We are blessed to have you."

She leaned toward him slightly. "We will have to wait until we have Bubble's assessment of my teaching skills before jumping to any conclusions. *Guten nacht*, Willis Gingrich."

"Good night, Teacher."

She walked away into the darkness. He watched until he saw her enter her house across the way. There was something attractive about Eva Coblentz that had nothing to do with her face or her figure. She was the first woman in a long time who made him want to smile.

He went back inside the house. The children were still eating. He took his place at the head of the table, bowed his head for a silent prayer, then reached for a bread roll. It was still warm. He looked at Maddie. "What did you say to your teacher that made her bring food here tonight?"

Maddie shrugged her shoulders. "I don't know."

"You must have said something." He took a bite of his roll.

Maddie had a whispered conversation with the empty chair next to her. She looked up and grinned at him. "Bubble says that she told teacher you need a wife who is a good cook."

He started coughing. Otto pounded on his back while Harley rushed to give him a glass of water. When he could catch his breath, Willis stared at Maddie in shock. "Eva thinks I'm looking for a wife?"

Maddie nodded.

Willis hung his head. Nothing could be further from the truth. There was no way he could keep his secret from a wife. Even if he found the courage to reveal his handicap to a woman again, there was still one pressing reason he had to remain single.

Amish ministers and bishops were chosen by lot from the married men of the congregation. At baptism every Amish fellow vowed to accept the responsibility of becoming a minister of the faith if he should be chosen. What kind of preacher would he make if he couldn't read the Word of God? The humiliation didn't bear thinking about. He would remain a single fellow his entire life. That was God's plan for him.

He turned his attention back to Maddie. "You were wrong to tell your teacher that I'm looking for a wife. I'm not. Now what am I supposed to do?"

Maddie lifted both hands. "Just tell her you don't want a wife. How hard can that be?"

Chapter Three

Early the next morning Willis hurried to get the cabinet pulls installed on Eva's desk and on the cupboards in the school. He glanced constantly toward the door, hoping she wouldn't show up until after he was gone. He had no idea how he was going to face her. He tried to convince himself that it had simply been kindness that brought her over with a delicious supper last night and not because Maddie had said he was looking for a wife.

Maybe he shouldn't even mention it except to thank her for the food. If he kept quiet, was he encouraging her or discouraging her? How could a six-year-old get him into hot water with her teacher in less than twenty-four hours?

He needed to make Eva understand that he wasn't interested in marrying without hurting her feelings or embarrassing her. She wasn't a giddy teenage girl. She seemed to be a mature and sensible woman. He would remember that and not beat around the bush with her. Maybe. Unless his courage failed him. These days it seemed in short supply.

He was fastening the final coat hooks in the cloakroom when he heard the outside door open. Maybe if he waited quietly she would go away without realizing he was in the building. So much for his courage.

He closed his eyes and listened for her footsteps. He heard her cross the room and open the drawers of her desk one by one. After a few minutes he heard her crossing the room again. Was she leaving? He held his breath.

"There you are. *Goot* morning, Willis. I didn't think you were about."

He opened his eyes. She was smiling at him from the doorway of the cloakroom. His heart sank. His courage had deserted him for certain. He couldn't meet her gaze. "I'm almost finished here. I'll get out of your way as soon as I can."

"You're not in my way."

He concentrated on installing the next hook. Only three more to go. "I know you must have work to do. Don't let me keep you from it." How did a man broach the subject of not looking for a wife like a rational adult?

"Is something wrong?"

"Nee." He pulled another screw from the large front pocket of his leather apron but fumbled the thing. It dropped and rolled across the floor to her feet.

She picked it up and held it out in her hand. "Maybe it's just my imagination but you seem upset."

"Nope." He snatched the screw from her palm. *"Danki."*

"Well, then, I'll let you finish so you can get home to your family. Please tell Maddie that I said hello."

He turned to face Eva. "I'm not looking for a wife."

Her eyebrows rose. She tipped her head slightly. "Okay."

"I know Maddie led you to believe that I am, but I'm not." His neck felt as hot as his forge.

"What makes you think Maddie gave me that impression?"

"You know. The supper you brought over." He rubbed his damp palms on the sides of his apron.

Her eyebrows drew together, creating a tiny crease between them. "I'm sorry, I still don't understand."

"Maddie told you I was looking for a wife who was a good cook."

Her eyes widened. "Oh, and you think I brought you supper to prove I had the culinary skills you are looking for? Sort of an audition for the position?" She covered her face with both hands and burst out laughing.

It dawned on Willis that he had made a huge mistake. He waited until she got a hold of herself. "This is the part where you tell me Maddie never mentioned I was looking for a wife who was a good cook, right?"

She broke into peals of laughter again but managed to shake her head. It wasn't the first time in his life that he felt like a fool, but it was the first time he felt like laughing about it. He chuckled. "You are a pretty good cook."

That set her off again and he was soon laughing with her. She wiped tears from her eyes. "I can see how it must have looked but I'm not angling for a husband with chicken and dumplings as bait," she choked out.

"Your rolls were fine, but the dumplings were gummy."

"They were not. I dare you to make better ones." Her mirth subsided. "You poor fellow. Has this been on your mind all night?"

"You have no idea. I barely got any sleep trying to figure out how to let you down easily. I'm going to have to have a serious talk with Maddie."

"She did tell me that you were a terrible cook and that Bubble believes you need a wife. I honestly made a batch of dumplings that was too large. I thought you and the *kinder* might enjoy them."

"The children all but licked their plates."

"I'm glad. Willis, I don't intend to marry so rest easy. I may be an old maid all my days, but I intend to put the years *Gott* grants me to good use."

He had a hard time believing she considered herself an old maid. He saw a mature, attractive woman who wasn't afraid to speak her mind or laugh at herself. He admired that about her. Any man would.

She folded her hands primly in front of her white apron. "In the future please don't hesitate to tell me if Maddie has shared something you aren't sure about. I shall do the same. That way we won't need to tiptoe around each other. Agreed?" She held out her hand.

He was more relieved than he could express. He took her hand. It fit as if it had been made for him to hold. "Agreed."

"One more thing. If you can quietly spread the word that I'm not interested in marriage I would appreciate it."

"If anyone asks, I'll let you know before I send them on their way. You might change your mind if the right fellow comes along."

Eva's fingers were swallowed inside Willis's large, calloused hand. She didn't mind the roughness of his skin. It was proof that he worked hard. She drew away reluctantly. "I appreciate the sentiment, but there is no need to check with me. I am excited to begin my career as a teacher and as you know, Amish teachers cannot be married women."

His nearness was doing funny things to her insides. He smelled of smoke and leather and something more that was uniquely him. She inhaled deeply and took a step back. "I do have work I need to get done. I've been going over the curriculum Samuel Yoder gave me. I have to say, seeing my duties laid out in black-and-white is daunting."

"Any new job is."

"You're right. I remember how much I enjoyed school. I want all my students to have the same feeling of happiness at gaining knowledge that I had. Maddie said Otto hates school. I hope that isn't the case."

Willis looked down. "Not everyone enjoys school."

His dry comment told her he was one of those. "You didn't? Why not?"

He still didn't look at her. "It doesn't matter. It was years ago. I've got work to do and so do you."

"You're right. I won't keep you from it any longer." Eva left the coatroom wondering why a man as bright as Willis hadn't enjoyed his school years. Maybe one day he would tell her but for now she had her own students to worry about. Willis left a short time later. The building felt oddly empty without him.

She sat at her desk and pored over her notes and lesson plans for each grade. The school board was thorough. She opened the enrollment forms and began to memorize the names of the students in each grade. If she knew the name, she wouldn't have trouble putting a face to it when school started. Looking through them she noticed she didn't have enrollment forms for Maddie, Otto or Harley. She would remind Willis the next time she saw him. She considered dropping by his home again that evening but decided against it. She had to draw a line between friendly and too friendly. Evening visits to his home were definitely out. Samuel Yoder would frown on that for sure and certain, but there was no reason why she couldn't stop by the smithy while he was working.

A loud grumble from her stomach reminded her it was long past lunch. She slipped her paperwork into the desk drawer, stood, stretched with her hands pressed to the small of her back and then walked to the window. A middle-aged Amish matron and several younger women were all getting out of a buggy in front of Eva's new house. Each of the young women had a baby in her arms. Eva rushed outside to meet them.

The women began unloading boxes from the backseat of the buggy. "Can I give you a hand?" Eva called out as she approached.

"Are you the new teacher?" the older woman asked.

"I am. I'm Eva Coblentz.

"*Wunderbar.* I'm Dinah Lapp. This is my daughter, Gemma Crump, and our neighbor, Bethany Shetler. Give her the *kinder*, girls, and let's get this stuff inside."

Gemma Crump deposited her baby in Eva's arms. "This is Hope."

The tiny girl with red hair gazed solemnly at Eva. "Hello, Hope."

Gemma turned away to pull a large box from the back of the buggy and carry it inside.

Bethany stepped up to Eva. "This is my *sohn*, Eli." She laid the babe in Eva's free arm and began helping the other two women unpack the buggy and carry boxes inside.

Eva smiled at the babies in her arms and chuckled. "Clearly, we are supposed to stay out of the way." She began to sway back and forth to keep her new charges happy. For the first time in years she was struck by the notion that she had missed out on something special when marriage passed her by. Perhaps that was why God had chosen her to be a teacher—so she could have dozens of youngsters to enjoy and look after. It was a humbling thought.

The sounds of running footsteps made her turn around. Maddie came rushing up to her. "What's going on?"

Eva nodded toward the house. "Some women have brought me gifts."

Maddie stared at the babies with wide eyes. "Do you get to keep them?"

Eva laughed at her expression. "*Nee*, I'm holding Hope and Eli while their mothers are busy."

Maddie took a step closer. "Can I hold one? Bubble has always wanted a baby sister."

Dinah came out of the house and motioned to Eva with little sweeps of her hand. "Come on in. You need to tell us where everything goes. Hello, Maddie."

Eva mounted the step and handed Hope to her grandmother. Bethany was waiting inside to take Eli from her. Maddie came inside, too. With both hands free, Eva parked them on her hips and surveyed the room. More than a dozen boxes took up much of the small sitting room. "What is all this?"

"When my husband, Leroy, told me you had accepted the job of becoming our teacher, we got together a few little things we thought you might need."

"A few little things?" The ad had mentioned a home would be provided. When she first opened the door and saw the kitchen appliances and a table with two chairs, she thought she would have to provide the rest. There was a bed and a rocking chair for the bedroom and a desk in the sitting room but nothing for the second bedroom.

"The men are bringing over the larger furnishings on our wagon tomorrow," Gemma said.

Dinah handed the baby to Gemma and opened the first box. "Kitchen towels and dishcloths."

"This is very kind." Eva was overwhelmed.

"We are thrilled to be able to start our own school," Dinah said. "The public school has been very accommodating to our students but as the bishop says, 'Raise up a child in the way that they should go and they will not vary from it,' and that means educating our *kinder* without undue influence from the outside. Okay, next box. Flatware, knives, canning jars and cooking utensils." Dinah looked at her expectantly.

"In the kitchen." Eva led the way.

Soon they were all unpacking boxes. The two infants were nestled together inside one of the larger boxes so their mothers would have free hands. Maddie knelt on the floor beside them, talking to Bubble and the babies nonstop. In less than an hour's time Eva had sheets and towels stored in her linen closet, a full set of dishes, a teapot and a coffeepot along with a pantry full of preserved fruits and vegetables and three new *kapps* in the style the New Covenant women wore. She would wear her old congregation's style *kapp* until she had been accepted into Bishop Schultz's church, but it was heartening to see they believed she would remain among them.

When everything was put away, Eva used her new kettle to heat water for tea.

The box she was most excited about was the one containing school supplies. "Maddie, come see this."

Eva lifted out pencils and rulers, colored chalk, paints

and plenty of wide-ruled notebooks for the children to write in.

"Is this for me?" Maddie asked.

"For you and all the school children," Dinah said.

Maddie picked up a box of crayons. "Bubble is really glad she gets to go to school. It's going to be so much fun." She put the box on the table and patted it. "I'm going to go tell Otto that this school is a lot better than his old one." She charged out the door.

Eva glanced at all the women. "*Danki.* I'm very grateful and so will my students be when class starts."

"We weren't sure what you would need," Bethany said, picking up her baby who was beginning to fuss.

"Sadly, I'm not sure what I need. I've never taught school before. From my own school days I remember the teacher wrote out the date and the arithmetic assignments for each of the classes on the blackboard first thing in the morning. After that she chose a passage to read from the Old or the New Testament. Following the reading, we stood up, clasped our hands together and repeated the Lord's Prayer in unison."

Formal religion was not taught in school. That was the responsibility of the parents and the church community.

Gemma chuckled. "That's what we did, too. After the prayer we scholars filed to the front of the room and lined up in our assigned places to sing."

Singing was an important part of the school day. It was all a cappella. No musical instruments were used in Amish schools or church services. "It was the same for me," Bethany added.

"I have a copy of *Unpartheyisches Gesang-Buch.*" The German songbook had been used in Amish schools for decades. "Will the bishop find that acceptable?"

"It's the school board that decides which books will be used. Hymns that are in common use will be fine. I used to allow the *kinder* to take turns choosing the hymns. Sometimes they would sing English songs and hymns. They sure enjoyed their time singing." Dinah smiled at the memory.

"You were a teacher?" Eva clasped her hands together. How wonderful to know there was someone she could turn to with her questions.

Dinah nodded. "Only for five years and that was a very long time ago."

"That's better than never. Where do I start?"

"Find out what they know." Dinah took a sip of tea from a white mug. "Parents in this community have made certain that their little ones understand a *goot* amount of English before the first grade because they were going to attend an *Englisch* school. That may not be the case for some of our new arrivals."

Amish children spoke Pennsylvania Dutch at home but school was where they learned English to communicate with non-Amish neighbors, merchants and customers. English and German reading and writing were both taught in school but only English was spoken there.

"You will need a teacher's helper," Bethany said. "My little sister Jenny will be happy to take on the task."

Eva had often been a teacher's helper. It had been her job to hand out readers to the three lowest grades and help any of the younger children with their schoolwork. Having such a position was the only preparation a young Amish woman normally had before becoming a teacher. It was the responsibility of the teacher to show her replacement what she needed to know for several months before letting her take over.

Eva remembered the oldest students working on their math or science assignments during the morning hours while the teacher listened to the small ones read. When the older students were finished with their work, they helped the younger children who needed assistance. In the Amish school she had attended, each scholar knew what was expected of them, and they did it without instructions. For many of the children it would be a big change from learning in a public school. They would all have to become accustomed to new routines. As would their teacher.

"You can expect mothers to sit in on classes to see what their children are learning for the first few weeks," Dinah said. "I'm sure you remember school outings."

She did but she hadn't considered that she would have to plan them. There would be picnics and special trips to be arranged. Eva sighed heavily. She wasn't sure she was up to the task. Becoming a teacher had seemed so easy when she was reading the want ad in her brother's home.

Dinah refilled everyone's cup. "This year will be our first Amish school Christmas program. I know the children and the parents are excited about that."

The Christmas program! How could she have forgotten about planning a Christmas program? There would be songs and poems to be practiced. Somehow, she would have to come up with a play for the children to perform. She grasped Dinah's arm. "How do I find Christmas plays and poems for the *kinder*?"

Dinah patted her hand. "Not to worry. I will give you the address for *The Bulletin Board*. It's a newsletter put out by Amish teachers. You can ask any question and get a dozen sound answers from teachers with years of experience and some who have new ideas."

Gemma frowned slightly. "I wonder where my husband is. Jesse was going to pick me up this afternoon. Hope has a doctor's appointment and Dale Kaufman was going to drive us into Caribou."

"Has she been sick?" Eva asked in concern.

Gemma shook her head. "Nothing like that. She was born prematurely, and she is at risk for developmental delays. Our midwife insists that Hope's pediatrician keep close tabs on her. So far she is hitting all her milestones, *Gott* be praised."

"*Gott* be praised indeed," came a man's deep voice from the sitting room. He stepped into the kitchen and dwarfed the little room. Eva had heard the expression a mountain of a man but she had never met one until now.

Gemma got up from the table with Hope in her arms. "I thought you forgot us."

"Never. I was sidetracked for a few minutes by a little girl who wanted me to push her on the swings because her brothers were all busy and Bubble said I could do it."

Eva grinned. "Maddie is adorable. I wish I could be like her."

Bethany laughed. "Because she gets to say anything and blame it on her imaginary friend? I can see the appeal in that."

"Are you going to take a meal to the Gingrich clan again tonight?" Jesse asked with a rumble of humor in his deep voice.

Eva shook her head, not the least bit surprised that Maddie had mentioned her gesture. "I may do some baking for them tomorrow. I was going to spread the word at the next prayer meeting that they need some ready-made meals."

The three women exchanged puzzled glances. Dinah

drummed her fingers on the table. "We took the family meals for the first week after they arrived, but Willis insisted he didn't need more help."

Eva could see him letting his pride get in the way of accepting help. "According to Maddie and Bubble he is a poor cook. Speaking of Bubble, what am I going to do with Maddie's imaginary friend in the first grade?"

"That you will have to decide for yourself," Dinah said. "I've known of a few Amish children with imaginary friends but never one that brought his or her friend to school."

Outside a car horn honked. Jesse took the baby from his wife's arms. The look in his eyes and his tender smile told Eva how much he loved his little girl. "We should get going. Dale hates to be kept waiting."

Dinah rose to her feet. "I should get going, too. My husband says my work would take half as long if I stopped talking. I hate to tell him it's never going to happen."

Eva follow her guests outside. She waved as Jesse and Gemma were driven away in a yellow pickup by a middle-aged *Englisch* fellow wearing a red ball cap. Dinah helped Bethany into the buggy on the passenger side and closed the door then turned back to Eva. "As a teacher you will be in a unique position to judge the welfare of your scholars. Our bishop is a kind man. If you feel a child's family may be in need, don't hesitate to mention it to him."

It was another aspect of being a teacher that Eva hadn't considered. She would be responsible for more than teaching the children to read and write and umpiring their softball games at recess. Could she do it all well enough or would Samuel send her packing?

She hadn't been in New Covenant for more than a few

days, but she would be sad to leave the friends she had made if she failed to please the school board. She gazed across the road and saw Willis shoeing a small black-and-white horse. It looked like Maddie would finally get to ride her pony. Willis looked up, smiled and gave a brief nod of acknowledgment in her direction before turning his attention to his task once more.

Of all the people she had met in New Covenant she suspected that Willis and his family would be the ones she would miss the most.

Eva went back inside the house. Her footsteps echoed on the hardwood floors as she crossed to her desk and picked up her favorite story. She sat down to read. Half-way through the first chapter she closed the book and laid it aside. The house was too quiet.

She crossed to the window that overlooked the street and opened it. She heard Willis calling his siblings in for supper. Harley and Otto were in a good-natured shoving match on the way to the door. Maddie walked behind, scolding them loudly as they ignored her. Willis admonished them to hurry. When they were all inside he shut the door, cutting off the sounds of his active family.

Eva slowly closed the window. She wouldn't get a cat to keep her company. Cats were much too quiet.

Chapter Four

The following morning was cool with a drizzling rain that dampened Eva's spirits. A restless night had weakened her resolve and left her wondering if she had made the right decision coming to Maine. Would she be able to provide the guidance and education the community expected her to deliver to their children? What if she wasn't suited to the job? What then? As Samuel had pointed out, her employment was only guaranteed for one month at a time.

Would that be enough time to learn all she needed to know?

If she lost the position, she would have to ask her brother Gene for the funds to return. She didn't want to go home with her tail tucked between her legs and admit her new adventure had turned out to be a folly just as her brother had predicted.

She had finished her second cup of coffee when a two-wheeled cart piled high with her promised furniture arrived. The driver hopped down with ease. His passenger, a large yellow lab-mixed-breed dog remained seated but watched her master's every move. A gangly youth sat on the tailgate.

The driver tipped his head toward Eva. "Good morning. I'm Michael Shetler. You met my wife, Bethany, yesterday."

"I did. And your new baby."

Michael's grin almost split his face. "Eli! He's a mighty fine little fellow except for his insistence on getting fed at any hour of the day or night." He gestured toward the back of the cart. "This is Bethany's brother Ivan, and the dog is our Sadie. She'll be at school most days because Bethany's little sister Jenny will be one of your scholars. The two are seldom apart."

"It's nice to meet you, Ivan. And you, Sadie." The dog barked once.

"That means hello," Ivan said, hopping off the wagon bed. "Where do you want this stuff?"

"I'll show you." She held open the door as they carried in a sideboard and had them place it in the sitting room against the wall across from the windows.

The door opened and Willis came in carrying a trunk on his shoulder. "Where?"

Her spirits rose at the sight of his smiling, soot-smudged face. She didn't stop to consider why he had such an effect on her. "At the foot of the bed. *Danki*, Willis."

She heard barking outside and saw Maddie playing tag with Sadie on the lawn. Willis stopped beside Eva. She grinned at him over her shoulder. "It appears Maddie has a new friend. Bubble may be jealous."

Willis stepped up beside her. "Nope, Sadie is an old friend. The dog was the first to visit us when we arrived."

Michael walked past them. "She likes to keep an eye on her flock. She might look like a lab, but she has shepherd in her somewhere. She visits all the children in the area at least once a day. Where do you want the bookcase?"

"A bookcase, how wonderful! Now I can get my books out of my suitcase. In the sitting room, please." Eva rushed into her bedroom and pulled a suitcase out from beneath her bed. Willis saw her struggling with it and came to help.

His eyes widened when he picked it up. "What's in here? Rocks?"

"A few of my books. The ones I didn't want to be without."

"Books about what?" He set it on the floor in front of the bookcase.

Eva unzipped the case, opened the lid and sank to the floor beside it. "About everything. My favorite books of poetry." She clutched several thin volumes to her chest. "The devotionals I enjoy, some adventure stories, even a cookbook. You're welcome to look through them if you want. You and the boys might enjoy reading some of them."

Willis held up one hand. "Another time."

"Where do you want the end table?" Ivan asked.

"Beside my rocker. This is very *goot* furniture. I assume it stays with the house for the next teacher?"

"I reckon so," Michael said. "The horse and cart are yours to use for as long as you need. You will want to invest in a closed buggy before winter or make sure you have someone who can transport you to church and such when the weather gets bad. One of our newly arrived families, the Fishers, are wheelwrights and buggy mak-

ers. I'm sure they can fix you up with a small buggy at
a reasonable price."

"You're welcome to use my closed buggy if the
weather turns bad before you can get your own," Willis said.

She was touched by his kindness and the generosity of
all the people she had met in New Covenant. "I will take
you up on that offer if I'm still here when winter arrives."

Willis frowned as he helped her to her feet. "I thought
you were staying for the entire school year."

"I hope I will be but Samuel Yoder made certain I
understand I am working on a month-to-month basis.
You should see the amount of paperwork he left me."
They all walked out onto the porch.

"Don't let old sour face fool you," Ivan said. "He's
happy to have an Amish teacher here. He has two grandsons who will be attending your school."

"I pray that sentiment continues. I appreciate the loan
of the horse and cart."

Michael walked to the horse's head and rubbed the
white blaze on his brown nose. "I brought hay and grain
for him. His name is Dodger. Where shall I put him?"

"Stable him at my place for now," Willis said.

"The church plans to hold a frolic next month and put
up a barn and corral for you," Michael added.

It was news to Eva but it made sense. Most of her
students would walk to school but some would need to
come by buggy or ride horseback. In the winter those
in outlying areas would arrive in horse-drawn sleighs.
The school would need a place to stable those horses.

She had been involved in many of the working par-
ties the Amish called *frolics*. When work needed to be
done, the entire community would set aside a day to

raise a barn, repair a home or harvest a crop for someone in the hospital. Everyone from the youngest to the oldest looked forward to the event and everyone helped.

After the men left Eva put out her books and then returned to her paperwork and lesson plans. She had a lot to learn before school started.

After two hours she decided against spending the day inside even with the drizzle. She took a cup of tea out on the porch and saw Maddie with Willis through the open door of his smithy. Without considering why, she grabbed a gray shawl and swung it over her shoulders then crossed the road to see what the pair was up to. The little girl was sitting on a stool, watching Willis pump the bellows to heat his forge.

"Maddie, you look so glum. What's the matter?" Eva asked.

"I can't tell you anything that Bubble says anymore."

"And," Willis prompted.

"I can't make up things for Bubble to say."

"That severely limits your conversation, doesn't it?" Eva winked at Willis. He shook his head as if wondering which side she was on.

Maddie leaned closer to Eva. "Bubble isn't happy."

Eva fought back a smile.

Willis kept his focus on his forge but glanced up at her briefly. "Did you get settled in?"

"For the most part. I should be working but I have decided to play hooky for the rest of the day. I can't look at one more lesson plan. May I try working the bellows?"

"By all means." He stepped aside.

She took over pumping a large wooden arm that worked the bellows. A few ashes floated onto her face and she brushed them away.

He glanced her way. "You'll have to pump faster. I'm losing the heat."

She picked up the pace. It wasn't as easy or as much fun as it had looked. The heat from the forge soon had her sweating. She cast aside her shawl. Willis turned a block of iron in the coals with a pair of long tongs. "When do you know you have it hot enough?" she asked.

"By the color. Iron glows red, then orange, yellow, and finally white when it's heated hot enough. A bright yellow-orange color indicates the best forging heat."

"Isn't it yellow-orange enough yet?" Her arms were getting tired.

"Almost."

She kept pumping until her arms were burning. "That's enough," he said.

Grateful to step aside, she let him take over. No wonder he had such muscular arms. "Now what?"

"Now I beat on the iron until I make something."

"What are you making?"

"A brake pedal for a buggy." He lifted the hot metal from the forge and placed it on an anvil. She watched him mold the metal into the shape he wanted by pounding on it. When it grew too cool it went back into the coals. In a surprisingly short amount of time, he had a new brake pedal ready to be attached.

"That is amazing. How did you learn to be a blacksmith? Was your father one?"

"Papa made furniture," Maddie said.

"Our *onkel* had a smithy near our farm in Maryland. He taught me the trade."

She tipped her head, glad for the chance to learn more about Willis and his family. "What made you move all the way up here?"

"The same reasons a lot of Amish folks are here. Farmland is cheaper than back home. Plus, I got tired of the *Englisch* tourists that came to gawk at us Amish. I wanted to practice my faith and my trade without feeling like I was a circus act."

"I know what you mean. I have this wonderful book that talks about how we strive to live apart from the world but by simply being Amish we are being drawn into that world more every year. Have you read it? I can loan you my copy."

He started pumping the bellows again. "I don't have time to read."

Eva swallowed her disappointment. "I understand. I reckon I've played hooky long enough. Thanks for letting me help in my limited way."

His mouth lifted in a brief grin. "You did okay. If you get tired of teaching, come look me up. I could use an apprentice."

She rubbed her aching forearms. "I don't think this is the trade for me."

"Can I help you at the school, Teacher?" Maddie asked.

"I would like that if your brother doesn't object."

"She is all yours. Remember what we talked about, Maddie." He leveled a stern glance at her.

"I remember." Maddie hopped off her chair and took hold of Eva's hand.

Willis met Eva's gaze and grinned. She marveled again at what beautiful eyes he had. She knew dozens of men but none intrigued her the way Willis Gingrich did. He was easy to talk to. She wasn't sure why she felt so comfortable around him. Maybe it was because she'd never had a friend who was a man before. "Maddie and I will be in the school if you need us."

He gestured toward several iron bars waiting to be made into something else. "I'll come get her when I'm done here."

"Don't hurry. Maddie and I will have fun. Oh, and before I forget, you need to fill out enrollment forms for the children. I'll need them before the end of the week."

His easy smile vanished. "Can't you take care of it?"

"I don't know their history or where they went to school before they came here. I'll need those records, too."

His frown deepened. He began pumping the bellows again. "I'll send Harley over to get the papers as soon as he gets back."

"Danki."

He didn't respond so she left and crossed the road with Maddie beside her, wondering if she had somehow upset Willis.

At the steps of the school Maddie looked back. "Whew. Bubble sure had a hard time keeping her mouth shut today."

Eva tried not to laugh but couldn't help it. "Why don't I read a story to you. That way Bubble doesn't have to talk and neither do you."

"Okay. I like stories. Do you have one about ponies? I sure wish Willis would put shoes on my pony."

"I thought I saw him shoeing a pony last evening."

"It wasn't mine. Harley brought it over from his *Englisch* farmer friend. Would you ask Willis to shoe my pony? He likes you."

Eva hoped that was true. "I'll remind him."

She saw he was watching them. She waved. He hesitated and then waved back. She entered the school with a light and carefree step.

For the next hour she read to Maddie and occasionally to Bubble when she couldn't be silent. Eva sighed when Willis came through the door to get his sister. She had enjoyed spending time with Maddie even more than she thought she would. The child had quickly wormed her way into Eva's heart.

"I was just about to teach your sister to write her name on the blackboard. Do you want to show her how it's done?"

He held up both hands. They were black with soot. "You don't want me handling your clean chalk and erasers."

"Okay, Maddie is spelled with a capital M, lower case a, d, d, i, e." She glanced at Willis. "Unless you spell it with a y or a single i?" She waited for him to clarify the spelling for her.

He shrugged. "Spell it however you like."

His comment puzzled Eva. "I want to teach her the correct way."

There was a thump against the side of the building. She glanced toward the windows. "What was that?"

Willis shook his head. "I don't know. Maybe a bird flew into the side of the school."

She frowned. "Do they do that?"

"Sometimes a bird will fly into a window by mistake. The first way you said. That's the right way to spell Maddie's name."

"Okay." She wrote the letters out and handed a piece of chalk to the child. "Your turn. All you have to do is copy what I've written."

Shattering glass caused Eva to jump and Maddie to

shriek. They all turned to look at the broken window. A fist-size rock lay on the floor amid the shards of glass. Eva and Willis stepped to the opening. She saw at once who was responsible. Otto stood a few dozen yards away with a bat in his hands. His eyes were wide with fear or shock. He dropped the bat and ran up the road.

"I can't believe he just did that." Willis scowled.

"It must've been an accident," Eva reassured him.

"Who did it?" Maddie came over to look out the broken window, avoiding the glass on the floor.

"Your brother, Otto. I'll bring him back to clean up this mess." Willis left the school and headed down the road with purposeful strides. Eva followed him as far as the front porch.

Out on the road a woman had stopped her buggy. She leaned out the door. "I saw the Gingrich boy break the window. He was deliberately hitting rocks toward the school," she called out loudly.

Eva's heart sank. She had assumed it was an accident. "Are you sure you aren't mistaken?"

The woman scowled, apparently offended by Eva's suggestion. "I am not. The bishop and the school board will hear what has happened."

"They will be informed, of course, but it would be best if the confession comes from Otto. He needs to face the consequence of his actions."

"Then he shouldn't have run off." She slapped the reins against her horse's rump and drove away.

Maddie came out to stand beside Eva. The child planted her hands on her hips. "Otto makes Willis want to tear his hair out every day. He's not sure what he's going to do with him."

"I'm sorry Otto and Willis aren't getting along. Otto

shouldn't have run away, but I can imagine he was frightened."

Maddie looked up. "He could have said Bubble did it."

"That would be a lie, wouldn't it? You don't blame something on Bubble if she didn't do it."

"I did when she knocked over my glass of milk last week."

"Were her feelings hurt? If you said I did something but I didn't do it, my feelings would be hurt."

Maddie scrunched her face and then beckoned Eva to lean down. She cupped her hands around her mouth near Eva's ear. "She's not real so she doesn't have feelings," she whispered.

"Willis will be delighted to hear that." Eva walked down to the lawn. "I think it would be best if you went home now, Maddie."

"Okay, see you tomorrow, Teacher. I'll practice writing my name tonight."

"That's an excellent idea. Have your brother help you."

"I'll have Harley do it. He's a right helpful fellow. Even Bubble says so."

As the child crossed the road, Eva turned her attention back to the broken window. It would need to be boarded up until it could be replaced. Poor Otto was off to a rough start at his new school.

Chapter Five

Willis found his brother sitting behind his smithy on a small, rickety bench that came with the property when Willis purchased it. He stopped beside Otto. The boy wouldn't look up. Willis gently kicked the bench leg with the toe of his boot. "I always meant to burn this in the forge. I just never got around to pulling the nails out. Besides, I like having a place to sit where no one can see what I'm doing. Do you know what I mean?"

Otto looked up. "Sure."

Willis shoved his hands in his pockets, leaned back against the wall and crossed one boot over the other. He stared up into the bright blue sky. "Do you ever feel like hiding out?"

"If you mean like right after I break someone's window?"

"I'm going to assume that today was an accident. Accidents happen when we are knocking rocks into the air with a baseball bat. Want to tell me why you were hitting rocks toward the school?"

"Because I hate school, but I wasn't trying to break a window. Honest. I just hit one too hard."

"I see."

Otto cast a sidelong glance at Willis. "How come you aren't mad?"

"What makes you assume I'm not?"

"Because when *Daed* was angry he yelled, a lot."

Willis shared a wry smile with his little brother who was still so much a stranger. "I remember that about him. It seemed he was always upset about something. Maybe I should say it seemed that he was always upset with me."

"After you left I became his headache. Harley could do no wrong and Maddie was always with our *mamm*."

Willis raised one fist to the sky. "'If I had a nickel for every mistake you made, boy, I would be the richest man in the county,'" he quoted in his best imitation of his father's deep, disgusted voice.

Otto chuckled softly. "He changed it to 'the richest man in the state' for me."

Willis slipped his hand back in his pocket. "I miss him. I should've come to visit more often. A week every Christmas wasn't enough to get to know you *kinder*."

"He talked about you a lot."

"Did he? That surprises me."

"He said you didn't have book smarts but you knew metal inside and out the way his brother did and you could make anything you wanted."

"He never told me that. It would've been nice to hear him say something good about me."

"Yeah, it would've been nice," Otto muttered softly as if he was lost in his own thoughts. He took a deep breath and sat up straighter. "*Mamm* said that he loved us. He just didn't know how to show it. Did you move away because he married her? Because she took your mother's place? That's what some people said."

"*Nee*, my mother died when I was a baby. I have no memory of her. I was happy my father found someone new. A few folks thought it was strange that he married someone so much younger but I didn't see that it made any difference. She loved him. I could see that. I moved away for other reasons that don't matter anymore."

"I reckon I gave the new teacher a reason not to like me today. Teachers always think the worst of a fellow."

"I don't believe Eva Coblentz is that kind of teacher."

"We'll see." Otto didn't bother to disguise his doubt.

"If you start at a new school with that kind of attitude, she may be forced to think unkindly of you. You need to give her the benefit of the doubt. She strikes me as a fair woman. I get it that you don't like school. I heard your *mamm* mention it often enough when I visited. I sure didn't like school."

That seemed to catch Otto's attention. "You didn't?"

"*Nee*. Like *Daed* said, I wasn't book smart." It was the closest Willis could get to admitting he couldn't read or write. He didn't want Otto to be ashamed of his big brother. He was the one the boys should look up to even if he was a poor substitute for their father. "I reckon you should board up the window and clean up the floor before going to tell the bishop what happened. I'll help you cover the window."

"Is the teacher going to punish me?"

"For what? For breaking the window or for running away instead of facing what you did?"

"Both, I guess." Otto rose to his feet. "Teachers can be mean. Do you think she'll believe that Bubble broke it?"

"She might, but I won't. Maddie may not be old enough to know the difference between truth and imagination, but you are."

"I was just kidding. I know I shouldn't have taken off without saying I was sorry. I guess I got scared. I'll have to pay for the new window, won't I?"

"That is only right."

"Okay, I'm ready to apologize."

"You will feel better after you do."

The sidelong glance Otto shot Willis showed he didn't believe his brother.

The two of them selected several pieces of plywood that Willis had stored in the horse barn. They carried the pieces to the school along with the ladder and were almost finished nailing the boards in place when Samuel drove up in his buggy. Eva came out of her house and crossed the lawn.

Otto glanced at Willis up on the ladder and then walked over to speak to Eva. "I'm sorry that I broke the window, Teacher. I didn't mean to knock that rock so hard."

"I thought as much." Her smile seemed to ease Otto's fear of her.

"Were you deliberately hitting stones toward the school?" Samuel demanded as he approached the boy. "Why would you do that?"

Otto shrugged but couldn't look the man in the face. "I don't know." He glanced at Willis as he descended the ladder and then straightened his small shoulders. "I guess I was mad because I don't want to go to school here and I miss my friends back home. I didn't mean to break the window. I am sorry. I'll clean up the broken glass. Don't worry about that."

Samuel's stern face relaxed. "I appreciate your honesty and I accept your apology, but you chose to do a foolish thing without thinking of others. Agnes Martin told me both your sister and your teacher were inside the building. What if that rock had struck your teacher or the broken glass had fallen on your sister? I know the loss of your parents must weigh heavily on your mind, Otto. Your move to our community was not your choice but one made for you by your brother. In all things joyful and sorrowful we must accept the will of *Gott* without question."

Otto stared at the ground and didn't reply.

"I spoke with the bishop and Leroy Lapp," Samuel said. "We will meet with you tomorrow morning at eight o'clock to decide your punishment."

A worried frown drew Otto's eyebrows together as he looked up. "Is that necessary? I said I was sorry."

"Our actions have consequences. It is important you learn that." Samuel nodded toward Eva and Willis and then returned to his buggy and drove off.

Eva laid a hand on Otto's shoulder. "Don't worry. Devouring wayward children is against the law. I'll be there to make sure they remember that."

Otto didn't smile. Neither did Willis. It had been years since Willis had been called before the school board to explain his actions, but he still remembered the sick feeling in his stomach. As much as he wanted to spare Otto the humiliation, he knew he couldn't.

Eva entered the school the next morning and found the broken glass had been picked up and the floor swept clean as Otto had promised. It wasn't long before Bishop Schultz, Leroy Lapp and Samuel Yoder came in. They examined the window without speaking to her, muttering amongst themselves. She hadn't been invited to sit in on the meeting but none of them objected to her presence. Finally, they moved a table to the front of the room, lined their chairs up behind it and sat down to wait. It was very reminiscent of her interview only days before. She wondered if poor Otto was as nervous as she had been that day.

She clasped her hands together. "I have a suggestion to make regarding Otto's punishment if you are willing to hear it."

"We're listening," the bishop said.

Eva explained her plan. The men listened in silence. When she was finished she sat on the bench under the unbroken window and waited.

Willis and Otto walked in at eight o'clock. Willis took a seat beside her. Otto walked over to stand in front of the school board with his straw hat in his hands. The men spoke to him in low voices. Willis leaned toward Eva. "Any idea what this outcome will be?"

"I did make a suggestion, but I don't know if they will follow it. I don't believe Otto meant any harm but destruction of school property is a serious matter."

"He already dislikes school. This isn't going to make it any easier on him. The families in this area are excited to have their own school. They're not going to like that a newcomer broke out a window before the first day of class."

"People will understand that such things happen," she whispered.

"I hope so."

The bishop gestured to Eva and Willis. They came and stood on either side of the boy. Willis laid his arm across Otto's shoulders.

Samuel Yoder put his elbows on the table and steepled his fingers together. "The window must be paid for. We don't feel it is right to penalize you, Willis, for something your brother did."

Willis gave a half smile. "I'll be happy to provide the labor to put a new one in."

"That is acceptable. The school board has enough funds in the treasury to replace the window, but that money should've gone toward schoolbooks and supplies for everyone, Otto. Some children may go without because of your carelessness."

"I can get a job and pay you back."

"Where? There are not many jobs around here for a boy your age. Your teacher has come up with a plan we agree with."

Eva smiled at Otto. "When school starts you will stay after each day for two months to sweep up, clean the blackboards, dust the erasers and take out the trash. At the end of two months we will consider the debt paid as long as you do a good job."

She glanced at Willis. He nodded his approval.

"Are we settled, then?" Willis asked. "I'm behind in my work and I must get back to it."

"Eva has an additional task for Otto today, but you may go, Willis." The bishop stood up. "We all have to get back to our work. Let this be the last time we meet this way, Otto Gingrich."

Otto nodded without speaking. The men filed out, leaving Eva alone with the boy. She squeezed his shoulder. "That wasn't so bad."

"I guess not. The bishop said you had something else for me to do."

"When my teacher wanted to make sure I remembered something important she made me write it on the blackboard one hundred times. I want you to write, 'I will respect school property' one hundred times."

"Now? Willis needs me to help in the forge today. I have to get going."

He started to turn away but she clapped a hand on his shoulder. "I want it today. The sooner you get started, the sooner you will finish and then you may go help Willis."

Otto shuffled toward the blackboard. She returned the chairs to their places and sat down at her desk and began to read through the first grade primer to see what she would be teaching.

"There's no chalk. Guess I'll have to do this later." Otto headed toward the door.

"I have some chalk here." She opened the top drawer and pulled out a box of chalk sticks. She held it toward him.

He took one from the box as gingerly as if it were a snake.

She didn't know why he was stalling. "Hurry up so you can help your brother."

He faced the board and wrote a lowercase i. He hesitated and pulled at his lower lip with one hand.

"Is something wrong? Is there a word you don't know how to spell? That should be a capitalized I."

"This is stupid." He threw the chalk into the corner and ran out of the room.

"Otto, come back here!" She sat stunned for a moment then rose and followed him out the door but he had already gone out of sight.

She crossed the street to the smithy. The sound of hammering told her Willis was hard at work. She stepped through the door but didn't see Otto. "Willis, did you see where Otto went?"

He held a red-hot horseshoe in a pair of tongs. He plunged it into a barrel of liquid. Steam hissed and splattered his leather apron. "I thought he was with you."

"He became upset and ran out of the schoolroom."

Willis pulled the shoe out of the liquid and examined it before looking at her. "Upset about what?"

Eva shook her head. "I'm not sure. I asked him to write that he would respect school property on the blackboard one hundred times."

"He refused?"

"He just ran out of the room without doing it. Do you know where he is?"

Willis carried another horseshoe to the forge and plunged it into the glowing coals. "I don't. Try looking behind this shop. He goes back there sometimes. Why would he run off? Did he say anything?"

"He said it was stupid." Eva wished Willis would show more concern but perhaps she was overreacting. Willis was Otto's parent for all practical purposes. She wasn't sure where her duty as a teacher lay. "I'm not going to let him get by with this kind of behavior. He will have to finish this assignment sooner rather than later."

"He will. I'll see to it as soon as he comes home. I know the boy. He won't miss lunch." Willis began pumping the bellows.

She took a step back, feeling dismissed. She certainly couldn't make Willis leave his work and go searching for his errant brother. She walked out of the forge and saw Maddie sitting on a swing in the school playground. Maddie spied her at the same time and gave a half-hearted wave.

Eva walked over to the playground and took a seat

beside Maddie in one of the swings. "I'm not sitting on Bubble, am I?"

Maddie shook her head but kept her eyes downcast. "She's not here. She had to go home for a while. She was missing her mother."

"I see." So was one lonely little girl unless Eva missed her guess. "You seem sad today. Is something wrong?"

Maddie slanted a glance at her. "Do you think the other kids will laugh at me because I talk to Bubble? Otto says they will."

"It isn't right to poke fun at another person. I will make sure everyone knows that. The Lord wants us to be kind to each other."

"That's what I thought."

"Did you see your brother Otto leave the school a short time ago?"

Maddie nodded and pointed toward the woods behind the building. "He went to see Harley."

"Can you tell me where I can find Harley?"

"Harley likes to visit his friend, Mrs. Arnett. She has a farm beyond the woods. You can follow the path through the trees, but Harley says I can't go that way because I'm too little and I might get lost in the woods."

Eva tried to think of a way to cheer the child. "You can come with me. Would you like to do that?"

Maddie shook her head. "I'm going to wait here for Bubble."

"I understand." Eva stepped out of the swing and headed into the woods. The trees grew close together and the underbrush was thick and leafy. Within a few steps she couldn't see the school building behind her.

Several game trails crossed the footpath, and once she took the wrong trail but quickly realized her mistake and returned to the correct one. Harley was right not to let Maddie take the path alone. She stopped when she thought she heard her name being called, but when it wasn't repeated she decided she had been mistaken.

After nearly half a mile she came to a neat farmstead with a big red barn and white painted fences. There was a young woman on her knees in a garden plot. Eva approached her. "Excuse me, is this the Arnett farm?"

The woman sat up and brushed her shoulder-length dark hair out of her eyes with the back of her wrist. "It is. I'm Lilly Arnett. How can I help you?"

"I'm Eva Coblentz. I'm looking for Harley Gingrich. Is he here?"

"He was but he left with his brother Otto a short time ago."

"I didn't meet them in the woods. Is there another way back to New Covenant?"

Lilly smiled and pointed toward the nearby highway. "I let them take one of my horses. You will find the county road is easier walking, but it is a little longer. Harley said he would be back later to finish mowing the lawn. I can give him a message."

Eva smiled. "Tell him his new teacher needs to speak to Otto."

"I'll let him know."

"Danki." Eva chose to walk back to the school on the roadway rather than tramping through the woods again. She could only hope that Otto had returned to finish his task.

When she reached the school, Maddie was gone. A black-and-white pony stood patiently at the hitching rail in front of the school. The door of the schoolhouse stood open. Eva stepped inside. Harley was sitting at a student desk in the first row. Otto was at the blackboard writing out his assignment. Eva gave a deep sigh of relief. She had been prepared for a battle of wills with him. It seemed that wasn't going to be necessary.

She watched and waited quietly until Otto turned to his brother. "That's all, right?"

Harley walked up to the board and began counting the lines. "Yep. I count one hundred. Now I got to get back to the Arnett place."

"Danki, brudder."

The boys grabbed their hats from the pegs on the wall and walked past her. "I'm glad you finished, Otto." She wanted to ask him why he had been so upset earlier but decided it could wait.

She walked to the blackboard, picked up an eraser and was about to rub out Otto's work when she noticed something was wrong. She looked at the first sentence on the board. It was clearly a different hand than the rest of the work. First sentence was neat with the words well spaced. The next sentence, while correct, wasn't neat. Some of the words were smooshed together while there were extra spaces between some of the letters. The more she looked the more she saw errors. Some of the letters were actually backward. A few words had missing letters. She put the eraser down. Otto's writing skills were far below his grade level. She decided to get Dinah's opinion and ask her what she thought.

She left the school and was walking toward her house when she heard Willis call her name. She stopped and saw him jogging toward her. He came to a halt a few feet away and rubbed the palms of his hands on his pant legs. "I wanted to apologize for being abrupt with you earlier. Please forgive me. I have so much work to catch up on. Otto is at home if you are still looking for him."

"He returned a short time ago and finished his work. I'm sorry I bothered you earlier. I'm new at teaching and I feel the need to panic at least once a day."

He gave a halfhearted smile. "I'm new at parenting, and I feel the need to panic all day, every day. I'm sorry Otto was rude to you."

"Come with me. There's something you should see." She led the way back inside the school and walked up to the blackboard. "This is Otto's work."

He looked at the board. "Okay?"

"Look at his writing."

"I am. He finished the assignment, right? If that's all I should get back to work."

"He finished by copying the sentences his brother wrote out for him. I don't think Otto could do it by himself."

"So he had a little help. I don't know what you want me to say."

"He has turned some of the letters around. He has copied all the letters but he hasn't divided them into the proper words. Right here he wrote, I willresp ect schoolpr operty."

"Okay, so his writing needs work. You will have the next nine months to help him improve. That's what a good teacher does, right?"

"Among other things. I don't think you are taking this seriously."

"Maybe I'm not. A few scrawls on the blackboard don't put food in the mouths of hungry kids. That takes hard work. Not busywork."

* * *

Willis needed to get out of the building. It felt like the walls were closing in on him. He didn't see what was wrong with Otto's work and he didn't want Eva to know he possessed fewer writing skills than his little brother.

Her gaze was piercing, and he flinched from it. "Reading and writing are not simply busywork, Willis. They are the foundation by which we learn everything from God's Word to the latest baseball scores."

"You're right. You're the teacher and the teacher is always right. Even I learned that in school."

"This isn't about who is right and who is wrong."

"I don't know why you are getting angry," he finished lamely.

"Because I get the feeling that you don't care about Otto's education or his future."

"I care that the boys will be able to put food on the table for their families. That will take farmland, which I don't have much of yet, or it will take a skilled trade. That is something I have and can teach them." He turned and headed out the door, wondering if he had revealed his own shortcomings. Eva wasn't a woman who could be easily fooled.

"Willis, wait."

He stopped at the bottom of the school steps. She was a tenacious woman, too. "I thought we were finished."

She stopped, framed in the doorway. Her green eyes brimmed with some deep emotion. "I don't mean to criticize how you are raising your brothers and sister. I know it can't be easy for you. I'm sorry for saying that you don't care about their education. It's no excuse but I find myself in uncharted territory. I may have crossed the line just now but I have no idea where the line should be drawn or how to change it. And that rambling explanation is my way of saying I'm sorry. I will limit my lectures to my scholars and try not to offend their parents or guardians."

"You're forgiven. If the boy has trouble in school let me know and I will speak to him about it."

"Fair enough." She arched one eyebrow. "I don't have many friends in this new place. I'd hate to lose the first one I made here."

"You haven't lost me. I live just across the road." He nodded in that direction.

A sliver of a smile curved her lips. "I should be able to find my way over if I try hard enough."

"I suspect you can be a very determined woman when you put your mind to something."

"I have occasionally heard my name associated with that adjective."

"Occasionally?"

"Perhaps *frequently* might be closer to the truth." Her grin widened.

"I'm not sure I've ever met someone like you," he said in amazement.

She crossed her arms over her chest and looked down. "A bossy old maid who speaks her mind isn't that rare of a creature."

"Perhaps not but I think you are one of a kind, Eva Coblentz."

Chapter Six

Eva watched from the doorway as Willis returned to his workshop. He might consider her unique, but she placed him squarely in the same category. In a society that valued the community above the individual and encouraged conformity, finding someone who wasn't offended by her outspokenness was rare.

She looked back at the writing on the blackboard. Her instincts said Otto's angry attitude was more than a simple dislike of school. Dinah was the person she hoped could help her solve the riddle of the troubled child.

Two hours later Dinah and Mrs. Kenworthy, a schoolteacher from the local public school, studied the blackboard carefully. Eva was grateful Dinah had been free on such short notice and had wholeheartedly agreed with her suggestion to call one of the local teachers to render another opinion. "What do you think?"

"Otto is eleven so he must be in the fifth grade?" Dinah looked over her shoulder for confirmation.

"That is my understanding. Harley is thirteen and will be a seventh-grader. Maddie is seven and will start the first grade."

Mrs. Kenworthy shook her head. "This is not the work of a boy in the fifth grade. It could be he has a learning disability."

"Could it be simple bad penmanship?" Eva asked. Was she making a mountain out of a molehill?

Mrs. Kenworthy's mouth twisted to the side. "I see more than that. For the most part he has the letters in the right order but he doesn't seem to realize that they aren't grouped into the correct words."

"For one boy in my former community, the problem was as simple as needing glasses," Dinah said.

"Aren't all Amish children given hearing and vision exams when they start school?" Eva asked.

"They are in Maine," Mrs. Kenworthy said.

Dinah turned away from the blackboard. "The vast majority of Amish students are tested by public health officials in their area, but not all. I'm sure it will be in his records from his previous school."

Eva held her hands wide. "I don't have them yet. The children haven't even been officially enrolled. I have reminded Willis that he needs to get it done but he seems overwhelmed with his new responsibilities. I hate to bother him with one more thing."

Dinah scowled. "Shall I have my husband talk to him about it?"

Eva shook her head. "We have a few more weeks before classes begin. If he hasn't turned in the forms by Friday I will speak to him again."

Mrs. Kenworthy tapped the writing on the blackboard with one finger. "The sooner you can address what is wrong with young Otto, the better off he will be. It appears someone is willing to help. The first line is in an entirely different hand. You think it was his older brother?"

"That was my assumption," Eva said. "I think he wrote out the sentence for Otto to copy and stayed with him until the assignment was finished."

"Speak to Harley," Dinah suggested. "Perhaps he can give you some insight. That way you won't have to bother Willis again."

"All right I will."

The three women walked outside. Dinah tipped her head toward Willis's home. "Is Maddie still conversing with her imaginary friend?"

Eva looked around for the child. "I'm not sure. I saw her earlier and she said that Bubble had gone home to visit her mother."

Mrs. Kenworthy laughed heartily. "Children do say the most amazing things. That is one thing we should warn you about. As a teacher you will hear many things parents never expected would be repeated in school. Do not be fooled into repeating it as gossip because most times the children have it all wrong."

"Thank you for the advice. I will take it to heart and seal my lips."

Mrs. Kenworthy walked down to her car. Dinah turned to Eva. "I had best get home. The bishop and his wife are coming over for supper this evening along with Gemma, Jesse and Hope. I can't get enough of my grandbaby. I praise *Gott* he let me live long enough to see and enjoy her."

"How did her doctor visit turn out?" Eva asked.

"Healthy and happy was the diagnosis the doctor gave Jesse and Gemma. Hope is still small for her age, but she is catching up."

Eva smiled with relief. "I'm glad to hear that."

Dinah started to walk away but stopped and turned back to Eva. "You are welcome to join us for supper. I made plenty of fried chicken, Gemma is bringing a casserole and Constance Schultz made some fresh apple pies for dessert."

"*Danki*, but I have more homework. I never knew there was so much paperwork involved in teaching."

"Oh, I remember those days. And the long nights getting everything ready for the first day of class. Being a wife and a mother was the fulfillment of a dream for me, but I do miss teaching at times. All those bright faces so eager to see me in the mornings. It is a satisfying profession and one that isn't always valued as it should be. Don't forget that other teachers, Amish and *Englisch*, are willing to help you get off to a good start. Several of the teachers at our public school have stopped in to tell me they will miss having Amish children in their classes."

"Thank you again for your help and tell Gemma and Jesse that I said hello."

"This coming Sunday is the off Sunday in our community so no prayer meeting. We will expect you to come visit us, and homework will not get you out of it." Dinah smiled as she issued her invitation.

Eva inclined her head. "I wouldn't dream of missing an afternoon in the company of you and your family."

Harley came strolling past the school, headed for home. "Good evening, Teacher. Good evening, Mrs. Lapp."

"Harley, can I speak to you for a moment?" Eva said.

"Sure."

"I have to get going. Let me know what you find out," Dinah said.

Eva turned her attention to Harley. She sat down on the steps of the school and motioned for him to do the same. "I noticed that you helped your brother with his writing assignment today."

"All I did was write it once. He did the rest."

"Maddie tells me Otto doesn't like school."

"Maddie talks to an imaginary kid named Bubble. I'm not sure you can believe much of what she says."

"Good point. Still, Otto has given me the same impression. Can you tell me why?"

"School is hard for him. Our last teacher never wanted to help him, so I do. He's smart. He's not stupid and people shouldn't say that he is."

"I would never call someone *stupid*. I'm sorry that your brother has been hurt by careless people. I will do everything I can to make Otto feel he is a valuable member of my class. At your last school did the children have their eyes checked?"

"Sure. And they checked our hearing, too. Why?"

"I haven't received those records, so I wanted to make sure the tests had been done." That was one reason she could eliminate for Otto's problem. "Has Otto always had trouble in school?"

"I think so. *Mamm* used to spend a lot of time helping him with his reading. *Daed* used to say he was just being lazy. Can I go now?"

"Of course."

He hopped up and jogged toward home. Eva remained on the steps. Mrs. Kenworthy had confirmed what Eva had thought. It seemed Otto would need additional help from her.

Harley stepped out the door of the Gingrich house

and cupped his hand around his mouth. "Send Maddie home for supper."

"She's not with me," Eva shouted back. The playground was empty and the child hadn't been with them in the school.

Harley waved and went back inside. Eva rose and walked the short distance to her house. She turned on the oven and pulled a turkey potpie from the freezer. She heard footsteps on her porch and looked at the screen door.

Willis pulled the door open and came inside. "Have you seen Maddie today?"

She tensed at the concern in his voice. "Not since this morning. She was on the swing set and said she was sad because Bubble had gone home to see her mother."

"We can't find her."

"Perhaps she's gone to play with some other friends. Where might she be?"

"She doesn't know many of the children her age yet."

Eva turned off her oven. "We should ask the neighbors if they have seen her."

"I don't mean to scare you. It's just not like her to wander off."

"I'm not scared, Willis. Concerned, yes, but Maddie is with God wherever she goes. He is her protection. Let me make sure she isn't here in the house."

"I will double-check the school." He went out.

Eva made a quick room-by-room search of her house and came up empty. She stepped outside and saw Otto and Harley near the trees. Harley had something black in his hands. They both came running up to Willis. Harley handed him a small black *kapp*. "I found it snagged on a tree branch a few yards into the woods. We yelled for her but she didn't answer."

Willis wadded the fabric into a tight ball in his hands. "She isn't supposed to go into the woods. She knows that."

Eva pressed a hand to her lips. "I asked her if she wanted to go with me when I went looking for Otto. She said no but she might have changed her mind after I was gone. I thought I heard someone calling my name once, but it wasn't repeated so I went on. What if she was trying to follow me?"

It was growing late. Eva's heart started racing. Maddie could have followed her into the woods. Why had she invited the child to go with her? "She wouldn't leave the path, would she?"

"She could easily lose her way," Harley said. "There is a second path that cuts across it and leads down to the river where some people go fishing."

Eva remembered the spot. "I almost went that way myself. What should we do?"

Willis handed the *kapp* to Eva and faced his brothers. "Harley, you and Otto take the path to the farm and keep calling for her but remember to stop and listen, too. Take it slow. Eva, you and I will drive over to the farm and see if she is there and check with our neighbors along the way to find out if anyone has seen her. I'll hitch up your cart."

"I have two flashlights in my kitchen. The batteries are brand-new. The boys should take them. It will be dark before long."

"Get them. I'll get your horse." Willis ran back to his property.

Eva fetched the flashlights and handed one to each

of the boys. Their eyes were wide with fear. She tried to reassure them. "I'm sure she is fine. Stick together. If you get off the path in the dark stay where you are. We will find you."

They took off and she hurried down to Willis's barn. He was backing Dodger between the shafts of the cart. Eva went around the horse and quickly attached her side of the harness. She climbed up to the seat.

Willis handed her the lines. "If she is there we will wait for the boys."

"If she isn't?"

"I will follow the path to the river while you bring the boys home. I pray one of us finds her along the way and she will spin us a story about how Bubble led her into the woods." He tried to smile.

Eva saw the effort it took and her heart ached for him. "Have faith."

"I'm trying." He climbed up beside her, lifted the reins and urged Dodger to a quick trot out onto the roadway.

Willis was grateful for Eva's calm presence beside him. He should have kept a better eye on his sister. He had no one to blame but himself. Maddie was too little to run wild the way he had allowed the boys to. Something would have to change.

When he reached the first house along the road, Eva hopped down and hurried to the door. She spoke to the man who answered her knock and then hurried back to the cart.

"They haven't seen her. They are going to call the warden service to get a search started. If we find her they'll let the warden know. They are going to head over to the farm in case more people are needed for the search."

"I don't even know them. They aren't Amish."

"There are *goot* people everywhere who are willing to help. Not all of them wear plain clothing, bonnets and straw hats."

"Sometimes it's easy to forget that."

A small smile curved her lips. "From time to time, I will remind you."

He looked at the remarkable woman beside him and thanked God she had chosen to come to Maine. He realized just how much he had grown to like Eva and how much her friendship meant to him. There wasn't anyone else he wanted with him during this crisis.

The car from the previous house went around them on the narrow road. Willis saw their taillights disappear over the hill. For the first time since he was a teenager he wished he had a car instead of a horse to get him where he needed to be quickly.

The next farm along the road belonged to a new Amish family in the community. The husband, wife and four grown sons were sitting down to supper when Willis pulled up. Ezekiel Fisher came out. "Good evening, Willis Gingrich. What brings you here?"

"My Maddie's missing. Have you seen her today?"

"*Nee*, I have not." He spoke to his wife and sons who had come to stand behind him. He turned back to Willis. "None have seen the child. We will help look."

"*Danki*. She was headed to the Arnett farm."

"We will search the woods between here and there in case she came this way."

Willis set the horse in motion. The sound of the animal's rapid hoofbeats on the pavement and the jingle of the harness were the only sounds as he urged Dodger to a faster pace.

Eva sat silently beside him. At last the Arnett farm lane came into view. The English couple from the first house and Mrs. Arnett were out on the stoop waiting for him. There was no sign of Maddie.

Mrs. Arnett stepped up beside the cart. "I've already called the sheriff department and the warden service. I also called a friend who is a neighbor to your bishop. He has gone to let the Schultz family know what has happened. The sheriff wants everyone to meet at the school and set up a search from there. Jacques Dubois and his wife will drive you back. You can leave the cart and the horse here."

"Otto and Harley are coming this way on the path."

Mrs. Arnett nodded. "I will get word to you if they show up with her."

"I thought I would search the path that leads to the river." Willis was reluctant to go back without Maddie. Somewhere she was lost, maybe hurt, frightened and depending on him to come and find her.

Eva laid a hand on his arm. "Maddie may already be home and wondering why no one is about."

She was right. He got down and helped Eva out of the cart.

Eva got in the car and scooted over, making room for Willis. In a matter of minutes they were back at the school. Willis called for Maddie and went to check in the school. Eva made a quick search of her own home, calling for Maddie as she went from room to room. There was no trace of the child. When she stepped out onto her porch she saw Willis coming out of his house. The look on his face told her what she already suspected. Maddie hadn't come home.

The sound of an approaching siren caused them to look toward the road. The siren stopped when the white pickup turned into the school driveway but the lights on top continued flashing. A tall man in a dark green uniform got out. "Are you the ones with a missing child?"

Willis stepped forward. "We are. Her name is Maddie and she is seven years old."

"I'm Sergeant O'Connor of the warden service. I will be in charge of the search at this end. We have more local law enforcement on the way to help. It will be full dark soon. Is there somewhere we can set up a command center?"

"In the school," Eva said, eager to help.

"I see that you folks are Amish. Is there electricity?"

"Nee." She shook her head. "But we do have propane lighting in the building."

"I have a generator," Willis said. "Will that work?"

"Perfect." Sgt. O'Connor looked toward the woods. "How much of the area has been searched?"

Willis gestured toward the trees. "My brothers are working their way through the woods on a path they often take to Mrs. Arnett's farm. Mr. Fisher and his four sons are searching between their place and her farm in case Maddie wandered north."

"And how far is this farm?"

"About half a mile as the crow flies," Eva said.

Sgt. O'Connor turned to face her. "What makes you certain that she went into the woods and not to someone else's house?"

Willis pulled Maddie's *kapp* from his pocket. "The

boys found this a little way into the woods along the path."

"Do you think there could be someone with her?"

Willis shook his head slowly. "I don't think so but I can't be sure. Maddie has been told not to go into the woods alone."

"Kids don't always do what we tell them. Don't worry. We're going to find her." Sgt O'Connor's sense of confidence buoyed Eva's spirits.

The clatter of galloping hooves on the road filled the evening air. A team of draft horses pulling a large wagon came charging into view from the valley below. The wagon was packed with Amish men, women and boys. Jesse Crump was driving. Bishop Schultz sat beside him, holding on to his hat. Jesse pulled the team to a halt. The passengers piled out.

The bishop walked up to the warden. "We are here to assist in any way we can."

Sgt. O'Connor looked over the crowd of volunteers. "Every warm body is appreciated. We're going to set up a command center in the school and plan out a grid search of the area. We have a K-9 search and rescue unit on the way, but it will be several hours before they can get here."

Michael Shetler and a young Amish girl pushed their way through the crowd to stand beside the bishop. The dog Sadie stood at the little girl's side with her tail wagging. The young girl gestured toward the dog. "This is Sadie. She can find Maddie."

The warden looked skeptical. "And who are you?"

"I'm Jenny Martin."

"Is your dog trained in search and rescue?"

"We didn't train her. I think *Gott* did. She rescued me when I was buried in the snow the winter before last."

Sgt. O'Connor smiled at her. "I appreciate the offer, but I'm not about to send another child into the woods even if she has a wonder dog with her."

"I understand your skepticism," Michael said. "But I think it's worth a try. The dog has proven tracking skills. I'll go with them. Willis, do you have something that belongs to Maddie? Something she wore recently?"

Eva handed over the *kapp*. Michael looked at the sergeant. "Can we go?"

The officer sighed. "I may be making it harder for our own dog with more scent trails in the woods but okay. Come with me. I'll get you a radio so you can keep in contact."

Another car pulled in behind the officer's truck. Lilly Arnett got out. Eva's hopes rose but sank when she saw Lilly give a slight shake of her head. Otto and Harley got out of the car and raced to Willis. "Did you find her?" Harley asked.

"*Nee*. I want you to stay with Eva," Willis said before joining Michael and Jenny at the officer's pickup where they were being outfitted with a two-way radio. Otto and Harley moved to stand beside Eva in front of the school.

She took one look at their tear-stained faces. "Don't worry. We're going to find her."

Neither of them spoke. She didn't doubt Willis's affection for his brothers, but they needed his comfort now, too. She wished she could hug them all. She walked over and touched his arm. When he looked at her she tipped her head toward the boys. "Your brothers are worried and scared."

* * *

Willis had been so wrapped up in his need to find Maddie that he hadn't given a thought to what his brothers were going through. It took Eva to point it out to him. She was better at looking after his family than he was. He touched her cheek briefly. "I'll speak to them. *Danki.*"

Harley and Otto stood off to the side of the school, looking as dejected and as tearful as he felt. They needed him. He wasn't used to being needed. He walked over to them, struggling to find the right thing to say. "This is not your fault."

"You should be yelling at us." Harley sniffled and his arms clasped tightly across his chest.

"Why?" Willis asked softly.

"*Mamm* always said we had to watch out for Maddie and keep a close eye on her. We didn't." Harley wiped his face on his sleeve.

Otto laid a hand on Harley's shoulder. "Willis doesn't yell. Haven't you noticed that? Maddie is going to say that Bubble got her lost."

Willis managed a wry smile. "I thought the same thing."

He pulled the boys into a tight hug in spite of his desire to start searching. Eva was right. They needed comforting, too. "I don't blame either of you. I'm the one who should have been keeping an eye on her. You are all my responsibility."

He glanced up and saw Eva watching him with a look of approval. He drew away from the boys. "I know you want to come with us but I need to know you are both safe so I can focus on finding Maddie. Do you understand?"

They nodded. He smiled at them. "Bring the generator over for the *Englisch* officer to use and help however you can but stay here."

Sgt. O'Connor, Michael and Jenny took Sadie to the place where the path came out of the woods. The dog cast about sniffing for a scent. Within a few seconds she gave a loud bark and strained at her leash. Willis joined them. Eva appeared at his side and handed him a flashlight.

She turned on the one she carried. "I'm coming with you. The bishop and his wife will look after the boys."

He took hold of her hand and tried to share how much her presence meant to him with a gentle squeeze as they listened to Sgt. O'Connor.

"Let the dog go first. Try not to get ahead of her. She may not be on the right scent so I'm going to set up a grid and have other searchers comb through these woods systematically. Be careful. Stay within sight of each other if you can but spread out and look for any sign of her. I'll stay in radio contact." He headed back to the school.

Willis reluctantly released Eva's hand, and their group began walking into the forest.

Chapter Seven

Eva missed the comfort of Willis's touch as soon as he let go. She curled her fingers into her palm to hold on to the warmth he'd left behind. In spite of the short time Eva had known him, she was starting to care for him on a level deeper than that of friendship. Her practical side put it down to the unusual circumstances they had encountered together.

Ordinarily, it would have taken her weeks to get to know Willis and the children so well, but they had been together frequently since she had arrived. She didn't dream that Willis returned her warmer feelings. She was standing by him as a friend because that was what he needed now.

She was happy if Willis found her presence comforting but to read anything else into his lingering touch just now was foolish on her part. She knew that. He wasn't interested in more than friendship. She suspected his reliance on her had as much to do with his insecurity regarding the children as anything else. She'd never had to worry about keeping her emotions in check in the past, but she would have to in the future where Willis was concerned.

Praying that Maddie would be found soon, Eva plunged into the woods behind Willis. The dark shadows of the pine trees swallowed the searchers' silhouettes within a few yards. All Eva could see were the bobbing flashlights of the people with her. The underbrush clawed at her clothes, and branches scratched at her face and hands as she trudged forward. Willis shouted for Maddie every few minutes, and Eva strained her ears to hear a reply.

They had been moving forward slowly for about thirty minutes when the light Jenny was holding danced wildly. "I found something," she called out.

Eva and Willis moved to join Michael and Jenny in a small clearing. Sadie whined, clearly eager to forge on.

Jenny held a scrap of fabric in her hand. She looked at Willis. "What color dress was Maddie wearing?"

He shook his head. "I'm not sure."

Eva shut her eyes and thought back to that morning. She remembered seeing the girl's black *kapp* and apron as she sat on the swing. She opened her eyes. "Blue, her dress was royal blue with a black apron over it."

It was hard to tell the color by flashlight, but Eva was sure it was the same material. "That's from her dress."

Willis grasped her hand and squeezed gently. "It means we're on the right trail."

The radio Michael carried crackled to life. "This is Sgt. O'Connor. Do you copy?"

"We hear you. Sadie is leading us away from the Arnett farm and down toward the river," Michael said. "Over."

"Do you think she is still on the trail of the child?" O'Connor asked.

"We do. Jenny found some torn material on a thorn-bush. Eva says it's the same color Maddie was wearing. We seem to be following a game trail. It's narrow and twisting. Between the darkness and the terrain, we are holding Sadie back. She could cover the distance much faster without us. Over."

"She's your dog. Will she stay with Maddie if she finds her?"

"She will," Jenny said with confidence.

"Willis, what do you think?" Michael asked.

Willis rubbed a hand across his chin and turned to Eva. "What's your opinion?"

"I think having Sadie with her will give Maddie comfort until we can reach her, but it's your decision."

Willis looked at Michael. "Let's do it."

Michael spoke into the radio. "We are going to send Sadie ahead. Over."

"Understood. The radio you have is equipped with GPS. That means we can track it from here. Can you attach it to the dog?"

"I can use my *kapp* and tie it around her neck," Eva said.

There was silence on the other end. Finally, Sgt. O'Connor came on again. "I'm sending two deputies on ATVs down to the river. They'll work their way toward you. The four of you follow the dog if you can. Your GPS says you are a quarter of a mile west of the river. Keep moving east. Do you have a compass? Over."

"We don't but I see the Lord has provided a big yellow moon rising now. We'll be able to keep it in sight through the trees."

Eva knelt and tied her *kapp* tightly to Sadie's collar

with the radio inside it. She prayed it wouldn't be pulled loose by the dense underbrush.

"Find her, Sadie," Eva whispered into the dog's ear. Sadie lifted her head and growled deep in her chest. Michael unsnapped her leash and she bolted away, barking loudly.

Willis helped Eva to her feet. Sadie's barking rapidly grew faint, but Eva could still hear her. Willis kept a hold on Eva's hand as they pushed forward. He shouted Maddie's name when Sadie stopped barking.

There was only silence. The rising moon gave Eva enough light to see Willis's worried face. Had it been a mistake to let the dog loose? If she had gone home, how would they know?

He pulled Eva to the top of a small rise. He cupped his hands around his mouth and yelled Maddie's name again.

"Hello? Sadie, stop licking my face. Hello?"

Eva threw her arms around Willis at the sound of that welcome reply. He hugged her tight as relief sucked the strength from her bones. "That's her. She's okay. Thanks be to *Gott* for His mercy," she whispered against his chest.

He let her go and they all hurried down the hill, shouting that they were coming. A snarl erupted in the dark ahead of them followed by Sadie's fierce barking and Maddie's scream.

Fear gripped Willis. "Maddie! Answer me." He tried to rush forward but the thick brush held him back. He finally forced his way through into another clearing. His flashlight showed Sadie standing on her back legs with her front paws on a dead pine. She began jumping and barking again. Ten feet over her head a black bear clung to the tree, glaring at them.

Willis heard a whimper behind him. He spun around. Behind a fallen log, Maddie was crouched with her eyes closed and her hands over her ears. Relief sent a surge of joy to his heart. He dropped to his knees beside her. "Maddie, it's Willis."

He didn't see any blood. Was she okay? He wanted to grab her up but knew that would frighten her even more. He reached out and gently touched her shoulder. She flinched, her eyes popped open and she launched herself into his arms.

"I knew you would come," she sobbed.

He held her tight as he struggled to his feet. "It's okay. I've got you. Are you hurt?"

"Bubble got us lost."

Willis caught sight of Eva standing a few feet away with her arms around Jenny. They were both smiling although he saw tears on Eva's cheeks. "Shame on Bubble. You should stop listening to her."

He carried Maddie to Eva. She cupped Maddie's cheek. "You scared us. Are you okay?"

Maddie nodded but didn't release her grip on his neck. "I got scared, too," she said in a small voice.

Michael had snapped the leash on Sadie's collar and pulled Sadie away from the tree. Jenny dropped to her knees and hugged the dog. "You are such a *goot hund*. I love you, Sadie Sue."

Willis knelt beside the dog and used his free arm to rub her head. "I think Sgt. O'Connor was right. You are a wonder dog."

Jenny beamed a smile at him. "I told you Sadie could do it."

The rumble of engines preceded the lights of a pair of ATVs as they made their way through the trees toward Willis and his group. Eva untied her *kapp* from Sadie's collar and put it on.

The two officers drove into the clearing and turned off their engines. The one in front pulled off her helmet and smiled brightly. "This looks like we've come to the right place."

Thirty minutes later Willis carried his tired and disheveled sister into the schoolroom. He was immediately surrounded by people of the community offering congratulations, patting his back and giving thanks. Sadie stood at his side, wagging her tail as if the excitement was all for her.

Harley and Otto pushed their way through the crowd to his side and locked their arms around him. "She's fine. *Gott* was *goot* to us this day."

Willis caught sight of Eva coming in. The smile she sent him made his heart leap. He didn't know how he could have made it through the day without her.

Maddie reached for Harley. Willis handed her over to him. She cupped his face with both hands. "Are you mad at me, Harley?"

"You know you weren't supposed to go into the woods alone and don't tell me Bubble was with you. She doesn't count."

"I won't tell you she was there, but she was," she finished with a whisper. "Willis is kinda mad at her, too."

He leaned toward her. "Only because you frightened

me half to death. You're never to pull such a stunt again. Is that understood?"

Maddie lifted her shoulders in a big shrug. "I didn't know I was pulling a stunt. I thought I was following Eva to the Arnett farm."

Inside the school, he found the women of his congregation setting out food along with napkins and coffee cups on a long table. He heard the hum of his generator outside the back door of the building. Sgt. O'Connor worked his way to Willis's side. He patted Maddie's head. "Best possible outcome. Once all the searchers are in, we will get out of your hair."

Willis gripped the man's hand. "I can't thank you enough for coming."

"The way I hear it you didn't really need us." He petted Sadie's head. "My deputy says Sadie found Maddie and treed a bear all by herself."

Maddie made Harley put her down. She walked over to Jenny. "Can Bubble and I come over and play with Sadie sometimes?"

"Sure, as long as that's okay with Willis. I don't think you should go anywhere without telling him first."

"Okay. *Danki*. I'm hungry. I missed my supper."

"We all missed our supper because of you, little girl." Willis patted her head. He looked at Eva. "Maybe your teacher can find you something to eat."

"As a matter of fact, I can. Dinah Lapp brought over a chicken and rice casserole. I think there's enough left to feed you both. But first a very grubby little girl needs to wash her hands and face. Come into the bathroom and I'll take care of that." She took Maddie's hand and led her to the back of the building. Willis hated to let

Maddie out of his sight, but he knew she was safe with Eva. She always would be.

Fortunately, someone had stocked washcloths and towels on the shelves in the washroom. Eva turned on the faucet. There wasn't hot water, but cold water would work just as well. She wiped Maddie's face and then her hands. She checked the child's arms and legs, finding a few scrapes and bruises but nothing serious. It could've turned out so much worse. She hugged Maddie and kissed the top of her head. "*Gott* was looking after you, little one. I will be forever grateful."

Maddie reached up to touch Eva's cheek. "Are you crying?"

"They are tears of joy." She brushed them away and straightened.

Dinah and the bishop's wife came in as Eva was drying Maddie's hands. Constance Schultz smiled at the child. "You had quite an adventure today, didn't you?"

"It wasn't much fun. I don't think I'll do it again."

Dinah and Constance laughed. Constance pulled a black *kapp* from the pocket of her apron. "I believe this belongs to you."

Maddie tipped her head to the side. "How did you get my *kapp*?"

"Michael Shetler gave it to my husband to keep for you. I'm afraid it has a tear in it."

Maddie poked her finger through the hole in the top of the bonnet. "Aw, this is my last one. Now what do I do? Willis doesn't know how to sew."

"Don't worry about it. I can make you another one," Eva said.

Constance folded her arms over her chest. "That's very nice of your teacher, isn't it?"

Maddie nodded solemnly.

Constance looked at Dinah. "What Willis Gingrich needs is a wife to take care of the *kinder*. One who can cook and sew for all of them. We may have to find him one."

Dinah chuckled. "It's been a while since I've done any matchmaking, but I don't think I've forgotten how."

Maddie gave her a puzzled look. "What is matchmaking?"

"A matchmaker is a person who helps a single fellow, or a single woman, find someone to marry," Eva said.

"Oh." Maddie cocked her head to the side.

Eva was amused by the concentration on Maddie's face. "I think your hands are clean enough. I'll fix you something to eat now."

Eva held Maddie's hand as they walked across the schoolroom. Maddie stopped and looked up at Eva. "Can anyone be a matchmaker?"

"I suppose."

"Could you be a matchmaker?"

"I could but I think I would make a much better teacher."

"Couldn't you do both?"

"I guess but I've never had the opportunity to try."

Maddie darted away from Eva and ran straight to her brothers. "Guess what?"

Willis held a plate of food in one hand and a cup of coffee in the other. Harley and Otto were both eating chicken drumsticks.

"What?" Otto asked.

"The bishop's wife, Dinah Lapp and Eva are going to help Willis find a wife. Someone who can cook and sew and look after us."

Eva closed her eyes for a second. "That's not exactly what was said." When she opened them she met Willis's thunderous expression.

"What exactly was said about finding me a wife?" Willis ground out each word as if he were chewing glass.

Chapter Eight

Willis glared at Eva. He had just endured the worst five hours of his life and now she was plotting to find him a wife. "I thought we had this conversation once."

"Dinah and Constance mentioned matchmaking in passing. They only want to help."

"And you didn't set them straight?"

"Lower your voice, Willis. People are staring. It's nothing to get upset about."

"Come outside with me." He started to walk away. He glanced back. She had her arms crossed over her chest and a stubborn expression on her face. He was almost too tired to argue with her, but he couldn't let this pass.

He walked back and leaned close to her ear. "Please step outside with me, Eva. I would like to continue this discussion."

"I'm not sure I want to."

"You started it."

"Very well." She stomped out the door. He glanced around the room. Everyone was looking their way, but he didn't care. He caught Harley's gaze. "I'll be back in a few minutes. All of you stay right here. Understood?"

The children nodded, their eyes wide at his harsh tone. He managed a reassuring half smile. "Finish your meal. We'll go home soon."

Outside he waited until his eyes adjusted to the dark. He spied Eva waiting for him on the swing set. He took a deep breath and forced himself to calm down. He walked over to her and sat in the swing beside her. Neither of them spoke for several minutes as he gathered his thoughts. He saw the searchers leaving in small groups, some in buggies and some in cars. Gratitude for the kindness of friends and strangers alike slipped across his mind, blowing away his anger.

He tried to read Eva's face, but the moon had slipped behind a passing cloud and it was too dark for him to read her expression. "I think I have already mentioned that I'm not looking for a wife. I'm certainly not going to marry just to provide my siblings with a cook, a babysitter and a housekeeper."

"I understand that. Constance and Dinah reached the conclusion that you needed a wife without a word from me. I wasn't sure how to respond so I kept quiet. Maddie was intrigued and excited by the idea. You know how she is."

He blew out a deep breath. "*Ja*, I know how she can be. So how do I stop Constance and Dinah from matchmaking on my behalf?"

"I have no idea. Meet some nice women but don't marry any of them," she snapped.

He chuckled at her prickly attitude. He leaned his head back and stared at the stars twinkling between the clouds drifting overhead. How had his life become so complicated so quickly? "I wish school started tomorrow instead of in two weeks. I'm never going to get caught up on my work at this rate."

"I can offer a suggestion but only if you promise not to bite my head off."

"I'm listening."

"I will look after Maddie and the boys for you during the day."

"I appreciate the offer but you have your own work to get done." He backed up, lifted his feet off the ground and swung forward.

"You will be helping me out in a way. I can ease into teaching gradually. I'll have three students instead of fifteen. I can give Otto some extra attention before school starts so he isn't as far behind, as well."

Willis braked to a stop. "What do you mean? How is Otto behind?"

She twisted sideways to look at him. "So much has happened today that I forgot to speak to you about Otto's poor writing. I had Dinah and Mrs. Kenworthy, one of the *Englisch* schoolteachers, come to look at the sentences he had done on the blackboard."

"Why would you do that?"

"Because I was troubled by what I saw but I wasn't sure there was a problem. They agreed that his ability to write is not at a fifth grade level. Harley says their mother helped Otto with his reading a lot but he hasn't mastered it. I was going to offer to tutor him."

Willis surged to his feet and walked a few steps away. "So he doesn't read well. So what? A lot of fellows have trouble reading. Once he's out of school it won't matter."

"Willis, reading does matter!"

Her shock made him see how far apart they really were. She was a woman who clutched a book of poetry to her chest the way a mother might cuddle a babe and spoke of it in loving terms. To her, someone who couldn't read was behind. Slower. A problem. She was too kind to call someone *stupid* but she thought it just the same. The whole time they had been searching for Maddie he thought of Eva as an equal, working as hard as he had to find his sister. He'd been comforted by her steadfast faith. He had forgotten just how unequal he would be in her eyes if she learned his secret.

He scuffed the dirt with his boot. "It's important to you, maybe. You like books and poems and writing letters. I don't have time for that stuff."

"Surely you have time for reading the Bible to the children at night? Seeing you seek the wisdom and comfort of God's Word teaches them to find it for themselves."

"Teaching our faith is the duty of the bishop and his ministers. I appreciate all you did today, Eva. Maddie and the boys have learned their lesson and so have I. I won't need your help or anyone else's to look after them. We'll take care of each other. It's been a long day. I'm taking the children home."

He half expected her to continue the argument, but she rose from the swing. "I'll go in with you to tell Maddie good-night," she said quietly. He glanced her way. The clouds parted, allowing the moonlight to bathe her in a soft glow. She was studying him with a curious expression on her face.

He wished he could read her mind. Which was a good joke. Even if she wrote out what she was thinking he wouldn't be able to understand it.

The following day was the off Sunday, and Eva was glad to stay in. She was too tired and sore from dozens of scratches on her arms and legs to visit with the Lapp family. She didn't see Willis except at a distance for the next three days. The children she saw playing together outside the smithy but they didn't come over to the school. Maddie waved once, but Otto pulled her hand down and shook his head. Maddie stuck her tongue out at him and ran into the house. Later Eva heard Harley shouting, "It's your turn to watch her, Otto. I'm leaving."

It seemed things weren't running smoothly at the Gingrich house.

Eva was only mildly surprised to find Willis on her front porch late Wednesday morning. She opened the screen door, unable to believe how happy she was to see him. She tried not to show it. "Hello, Willis. What brings you here today?"

"I have to pick up some iron bars in town. I thought you might like to ride along with the children and me and see some different parts of the North Country."

She sensed there was more to his sudden invitation than he was letting on. Her curiosity got the better of her. "I would like that."

"*Goot.* I'll bring up the wagon." His look of relief almost made her laugh.

Maddie was sitting on the wagon seat when he pulled up in front of Eva's house. The boys were sitting on the floor of the wagon behind the bench seat. Maddie grinned from ear to ear. "Hi, Teacher. We're going to town. I'm so glad you can come with us. Bubble has been asking to see you for days."

"That's no lie," Otto said drily from his place behind her.

Maddie nodded. "Yep, Bubble has been asking day

and night if we could visit you. Willis is tired of her talking about it."

Willis leaned across Maddie and held out his hand to help Eva up. She cocked an eyebrow as she gazed at his embarrassed expression. "Is that so?"

"Yep, it's so," Maddie continued as she scooted over to make room for Eva. "He's going to buy some material so I can have a new dress and a new *kapp*, too."

"Has your brother learned to sew?" Eva had trouble keeping a straight face.

"I don't know." Maddie turned to look at Willis. "Can you?"

"*Nee*, but I thought I might be able to bribe someone I know into doing it with a nice lunch in town."

"That's rather presumptuous of you, isn't it?" Eva wasn't about to let him off the hook so easily.

"Desperate times call for desperate measures," he muttered.

Maddie lifted the front of her apron. "Harley sewed this patch on my dress." The stitches were uneven, and the fabric was puckered.

"I told you not to tell anyone." Harley's annoyed voice caused Eva to look back at him.

"It's nothing to be ashamed of, Harley," she said softly. "Your sister is blessed to have such a caring brother."

"Willis made me do it." Clearly, Harley hadn't enjoyed the task.

"Otto fixed supper last night," Maddie said with a wide smile. "He made grilled cheese sandwiches. Bubble doesn't like burnt cheese and bread."

"Bubble can cook her own supper from now on," Otto shouted.

"You made her cry." Maddie's lower lip trembled as she cuddled her imaginary friend.

"She's not real," Harley snapped.

"Enough!" Willis's commanding tone silenced everyone.

Eva cleared her throat. "It sounds like you have had a trying few days, Mr. Gingrich."

Maddie leaned closer to Eva. "He broke his best hammer, too," she whispered. "Did you matchmake him a wife yet?"

"Nee," Eva whispered back. "Willis doesn't want a wife."

"He needs one," Harley muttered.

"I can turn this wagon around and take you all home," Willis threatened, proving he had heard Harley.

Maddie looked appalled. "But then Bubble won't get to eat ice cream."

Willis fixed his gaze on Eva. "Is the offer to watch these darling children during the day still open?"

Maddie pressed her hands together as she looked at Eva. "Please, please, please."

"Ja, my offer is still open."

"Does that include lunches?" Otto asked hopefully.

"I think I can manage to feed you, as well."

"Wunderbar!" The relief in Otto's tone made Eva laugh.

Willis gave her a wry smile. "I think I may owe you my life. Their joy at finding their lost sister has worn off."

"Because she is back to being an annoying pest," Otto said.

Maddie rounded on him. "I'm not a pest. You just

don't like playing with Bubble. You wanted her to stay lost."

Eva slipped her arms around Maddie. "We are all glad you didn't stay lost. Right, boys? They cried when they couldn't find you."

"They did?" Maddie wasn't sure she believed that.

"They did," Willis assured her. "Your brothers love you. You should try being nicer to them. They don't have to play with you all day. They have things they like to do."

Maddie pressed her head against Eva's side. "But I don't like being alone. What if the bear comes to get me?" Her voice broke on a sob.

Eva met Willis's astonished gaze. She could see this was the first time he had heard about Maddie's new fear.

Harley stood up and tugged on the ribbon of Maddie's *kapp*. "No bear will come within a mile of our place."

"That's right," Willis said. "They don't like fire, and I always have a fire going in the smithy."

Maddie looked up at Eva. "Is that true?"

Eva nodded. "That is true. I read it in a book once. Bears won't come near a fire."

It took them a while to restore Maddie's good humor, but she was happily talking about starting school in a new dress by the time they reached the nearby town of Fort Craig. The foundry was located on the north end beside the river.

Eva and the children waited in the wagon while Willis purchased his iron bars. He spent the next twenty minutes loading them with Harley and Otto's help.

Willis climbed up to the wagon seat when they were done. The boys sat on the sideboards of the back. Willis looked at Eva. "Are you hungry? There's a nice restaurant in town if you'd like to try it? It's buffet style."

"I'm always happy to sample someone else's cooking."

They drove the wagon to an empty lot and left the horses there while they walked to the restaurant. It was busy inside, but the waitress was able to seat them at a small table in the back corner. The room was cozy with red-and-white-checked tablecloths and lace curtains on the windows.

Most of the patrons were *Englisch* families enjoying an afternoon out. Some of them gawked at Eva and Willis in their plain clothing.

Willis followed Eva as she filled her plate and helped Maddie make her choices. After Eva sat down, Willis and the boys returned with two heaping plates of food each.

Eva looked at them in amazement. "Can you really eat all that?"

"This will be a good start," Harley declared.

Otto licked his lips. "Did you see the dessert bar? I'm hankering for a big piece of that lemon cake."

"The owner of this place is going to lose money on us," Eva said.

Willis gestured toward Eva's plate. "You and Maddie eat like birds. We balance each other."

Eva treasured the warmth spilling through her veins as he smiled at her. They did balance each other in many ways. She dropped her gaze to her hands folded on the table. She had to be careful or she would find herself in trouble. Sitting with his family didn't make her a part of his family. She already liked Willis and the children way too much. He wasn't interested in finding a wife, and she had a job to do. That was what she needed to focus on.

* * *

Willis bowed his head and began silently reciting the *Gebet Nach Dem Essen*, the Prayer Before Meals.

O Lord God, heavenly Father, bless us and these Thy gifts, which we accept from Thy tender goodness. Give us food and drink also for our souls unto life eternal, that we may share at Thy heavenly table, through Jesus Christ. Amen.

He followed it with the Lord's Prayer, also prayed silently, knowing he had much to be thankful for.

He raised his head to signal the end of the prayer for Eva and the kids. The boys began eating like they would never see food again.

Eva pressed a hand to her lips to stifle a smile.

Willis cleared his throat. "You'll founder if you don't slow down."

Otto shot him a questioning look. "I thought only horses could founder from eating too much grain?"

Willis rolled his eyes. "Don't put it to the test. Slow down and enjoy your food."

"It smells like our house used to before *Mamm* died," Harley said. Otto and Maddie nodded.

The aroma of warm bread and pot roast filled the air. Willis thought back to the food his stepmother used to make. Roast beef, roast pork, fried chicken and potatoes, schnitzel with sauerkraut, all served piping hot from her stove, with fresh bread smeared with butter and bowls of vegetables from her garden. He never gave a thought to how much work she had done in making those meals until he had tried to feed his siblings three times a day. A few evenings he had caught the same delicious aromas drifting from Eva's place. Her house smelled like a home should. The children were going to enjoy eating at her place.

The thought brought him back to why she was here with him. "I can't pay you much for watching the children. You'll have to wait until after the potato harvest for any kind of payment, I'm afraid."

She waved aside his suggestion. "I refuse to take money. I have already told you having the children will benefit me."

"All right. When shall I bring them over?"

"First thing in the morning?"

"Agreed."

The rest of the meal passed pleasantly. When they finished, they crossed the street to the fabric store where Eva picked out a soft green cotton for Maddie's new dress and a yard of white material to make her new *kapps*. Willis didn't mind the expense. Seeing Eva's enjoyment while shopping with his sister and Maddie's bright smile was worth the cost.

Back at the wagon he climbed aboard and stowed the packages before reaching down to help Eva up. A sizzle of awareness spread through him as his hand engulfed her slender fingers. The desire to pull her closer shocked him. Her gaze flashed to his. Her green eyes widened. Was she feeling the same sensation? Her fingers were so delicate. Her skin was soft and smooth, not calloused like his. It was a pointed reminder of just how different they were.

It was something he shouldn't forget. Her world was filled with books, poetry and beautiful words to describe the world and the people in it. His world was hot glowing charcoal, heat, smoke and the deafening ring of a hammer striking iron. There was nothing soft or gentle about it.

She stepped up quickly and sat down, pulling her hand away from him. There was something about Eva that left him constantly off balance. He rubbed his palm on his pant leg, determined to erase the feelings from his mind, too. The sooner he got back to his smoldering pit, the sooner he could forget about the quiet magnetism that seemed to draw him toward her.

The children were quiet for a change on the way home. He glanced toward Eva a few times, but she seemed more interested in the scenery than having a conversation. It was just as well. He had no idea what to say to her. He dropped her off at her house and guided the horses to the back of his smithy. Harley stayed to help him unload while Otto and Maddie headed to the house.

Otto came back a few moments later with a piece of paper in his hand. He held it out to Willis. "Someone left this on our door."

Willis pulled another length of iron from the wagon bed to hide his shaking hands as his heart began racing. "Read it."

"It's for you." Otto waved it as if Willis couldn't see he held it.

"I've got to get this unloaded. Is it important?"

"I don't want to read your stuff. You take it."

Harley tossed his length of pipe on the pile, snatched the message from Otto and scanned it. "It's from Bishop Schultz. He says he'll be back to talk to you tomorrow at noon."

Willis let out the breath he'd been holding. "Does he say what about?"

"Nope."

"Danki." He began unloading his iron with renewed vigor. His secret was safe for now. He glanced up and found Harley watching him with an odd expression on his face. Willis swallowed hard. How much longer would it be before one of his brothers learned the truth? He cringed at the thought. What would they think of him then? What would Eva think of him?

The following morning Otto and Maddie tried to hurry out of the house before breakfast, but Willis stopped them at the door. He glanced at the empty wire egg basket on the counter. "Maddie, did you do your chores this morning?"

She looked up at him with wide, innocent eyes. "Not yet."

He frowned at Otto. "Have you fed the chickens and geese?"

"I thought I'd do it after breakfast."

"No one is going to Eva's house until their chores are finished. I will have breakfast ready for you by then."

Maddie frowned. "But Eva might have something better than you make."

"What's wrong with my oatmeal?"

"Nothing," Otto said. "If you like oatmeal."

Willis stifled a grin. He was getting tired of oatmeal, too, but it was a good, hot meal that would last a fella until noon or later. Eva was willing to make their lunches. He wasn't going to test her patience by sending the kids over for breakfast, too. He sent them on their way a short time later. Harley was the only one who finished his bowl of cereal.

Willis managed to catch up on some of his back-logged orders for potato-digging parts and cultivator shovels before the bishop showed up in his buggy. He wiped his hands on a rag. "Welcome, Bishop. What can I do for you today?"

Bishop Schultz glanced around. "Where are your brothers and sister?"

"Eva is keeping an eye on them today. Why?"

"The children are why I'm here. After Maddie went missing, several of the women in the church have expressed concerns about your ability to care for them."

Harley was reading in Eva's sitting room while Maddie and Otto were decorating sugar cookies in the kitchen when she heard someone at her door. She opened it and saw Willis with both arms braced on either side of the door and a fierce scowl on his face. "Were you in on this?"

She leaned back. "In on what?"

"On the bishop's visit to my home today."

She could see he was angry. She stepped out on the porch, forcing him to let her pass, and closed the door. "Willis, I don't know what you are talking about."

"The bishop wanted me to know that some of the women in the community are worried that I'm not raising my siblings right."

She slapped a hand to her chest. "I never said anything of the sort to the bishop or anyone else. I think you're trying hard to replace their mother and father. It can't be easy for you, but you're doing okay."

He raked a hand through his hair. "You're wrong there. I know I'm doing a lousy job. I never expected to have the children living with me."

"What exactly did the bishop say?"

Willis shot a sour glance her way. "He suggested I find a wife."

"Oh. I'm well aware of your aversion to matrimony."

"My what?"

She waved one hand. "Aversion. It means you can't stand the idea."

"Why didn't you just say that? Why do you have to use big words?"

She folded her arms across her middle. "Because I like the sound of them. Words are the decorations of life. Good words are like frosting on a cake. Exemplify. Emancipate. Enlighten. They sound magnificent because they are magnificent."

"Do you even know what they mean?"

"Of course I do, but I digress, which means I got off the subject."

"I'm not completely ignorant."

She took a step closer and gazed intently into his eyes. "I never thought that for a minute. This will blow over when school starts and the children are occupied all day. The good ladies of the church will find a new mission."

"Maybe they are right. Maybe the kids would be better off with someone else."

"You can't mean that."

"Maybe I do." He turned and walked away. Eva longed to call him back, but she knew he had to decide what was best for his family by himself.

She went back into the kitchen and saw Harley had joined the younger children there. He was writing on a piece of paper while the other two looked on. "Is this all?" he asked them.

Maddie and Otto nodded. Harley handed them the paper. "I think it's a dumb idea but here it is."

Maddie grinned as Eva walked in. "Teacher, we have a list for you."

Eva put aside her concern for Willis. "A list for what?"

"To help you matchmake a nice wife for Willis."

Eva narrowed her eyes and hooked her thumb toward the door. "Did you hear us talking outside?"

They all shook their heads. Eva took a seat at the table. "What's on the list?"

"She has to be pretty," Harley said. "That's my only suggestion."

"And not old," Otto added.

Eva tipped her head to the side. "What do you consider old?"

The kids exchanged looks. "A hundred," Maddie offered.

"That's really old," Harley said. "Maybe fifty. Like you."

Eva bit down on her upper lip. "Under fifty. What else, Harley?"

"That was my only suggestion. Ask them."

"Well?" She looked at Maddie and Otto.

Maddie held the list out like she was reading it. "She has to be a good cook. She has to smell nice. She has to have a dog. What else did we say, Harley?"

"She needs to sew and not make us take too many baths," Otto finished.

Eva took the list from Maddie. "This is a tall order. It may take me a while to matchmake someone with all these qualifications. What happens if Willis doesn't like the woman I find?"

Maddie scrunched her face in deep thought. She brightened suddenly. "We could get our own dog."

Eva folded the list and put it in her apron pocket. "Let's not tell Willis about this. He has a lot on his mind today." Someday she would share the note with him and they would both laugh about it. Now wasn't that time.

Harley came into the barn as Willis was finishing feeding and grooming the horses that evening. He let himself out of Dodger's stall. "Where have you been?"

"The Arnett place."

Willis hung up his brush and currycomb. "What are you doing over there every day?"

"Chores mostly. Lilly always has a list of things for me to do."

"You've been gone so much I was beginning to think you had a girlfriend."

Harley blushed bright red. "I don't and I don't want one."

Willis snatched off his brother's hat and ruffled his hair. "*Goot.* You're growing up too fast as it is."

"I didn't get much choice in the matter."

"No, you didn't." Willis slipped his arm around his brother's shoulders. Otto and Maddie came out of the house. Willis gestured for them to come over. They gathered in front of him. Maybe the children would be better off with someone else. He had to at least consider the possibility.

He could give them the choice. "The bishop came to see me today."

"What did he want?" Otto asked.

"He's concerned that I'm not raising the three of you properly. What do you think?"

Harley hooked his thumbs in his suspenders and stared at the ground. "You're doing okay."

"All that praise will go to my head." Willis bent sideways to see his brother's face. "How about the truth?"

Harley shrugged. "There are things you could improve."

"Enlighten me," Willis said, choosing one of Eva's words. He sat down on a bale of hay beside the barn door.

"I guess we want to feel like a family again. We can take on more chores. We aren't babies." Harley's voice trailed away.

Willis looked around at three unhappy faces. "The bishop could find you another family to live with if that's what you want." He barely got the words out of his tight throat.

Otto glared at him. "Is that what you want?"

Willis wanted his old life back, didn't he? Where he didn't have to be concerned about anyone but himself. Where he was never a disappointment to anyone else. He cleared his throat. "I love you. I want what's best for you."

Maddie climbed onto the bale beside him and rested her head against his arm. "Bubble doesn't want to live anywhere else."

Harley glanced at Otto. "Neither do we."

"I miss the things *Mamm* and *Daed* used to do with us," Maddie said.

"What things?" Willis asked.

"*Mamm* used to read us Bible stories at night. And she used to tuck me in real tight. You don't tuck very well."

"I can learn to do better. Why haven't you said anything before?"

They looked at each other. Maddie sighed deeply. "I was scared you wouldn't like me and you might send me away."

He put his arm around her. "Nope. Not going to happen. I'm not sending Otto away. I'm not sending Harley away and I'm not sending Bubble or you away. You are my family and you can stay with me until you have families of your own. Okay?"

They all nodded and smiled. Willis swallowed the lump in his throat. "Otto, you're in charge of Dodger, my buggy horse and the draft horses. Feed them and make sure they have water. Keep them groomed, keep their stalls clean and make sure Dodger gets plenty of exercise. We don't want him to act up when the teacher is driving him."

"Can I drive him?" Otto asked hopefully.

"Okay. You're old enough to handle the reins. Maddie, you will feed the chickens and geese every morning and gather the eggs. Plus, you will sweep the kitchen every day after breakfast. Got it?"

She nodded. "Got it."

Willis looked at Harley. Maybe this was the time he should confess how dimwitted he was but his insecurity ran deep down into his bones. "Harley, I'm putting you in charge of bringing in the mail, reading it and letting me know what things are important."

"Eva needs our enrollment forms filled out," Harley said. "I can do that."

"I almost forgot about those forms. It would be great if you could do that for me." He wanted to hug the boy.

"It will be up to you to find stories and prayers to read to us in the evening. Eva has lots of books. She's offered to loan us some and I think we should take her up on that."

Maddie's eyes lit up. "Oh, do you think she has *Rebecca of Sunnybrook Farm*?"

"I'm not sure. You should ask her. Eva also needs some help learning to be a teacher. She's never done it before. She would like you, Maddie, and you, Otto, to be her first students."

Otto scowled. "I don't want to go to school. School is stupid."

"I felt that way about school when I was your age and my opinion has never changed, but I didn't have a teacher as nice as Eva. I think you should give her a chance, Otto."

The boy stared at his bare feet and drew a circle with his big toe in the dirt. "I'll go but I won't like it."

Maddie got off the bale and took Otto's hand. "She can make it fun. You'll see."

Willis stood up. "All right, this family meeting is officially over. I think we should have a family meeting every week to make sure we're on the right track. Bishop Schultz is worried that I can't take care of you. So I think we're going to have to take care of each other. We're going to be a family team."

Harley grinned and held out his fist. "This is how the team does it. Everybody put your hand in." Maddie had to stand on the bale, but they all stacked their hands on top of each other's.

"Go, Gingrich team," Harley declared. The boys cheered as they tossed their hands in the air. Maddie jumped up and down, clapping her hands.

Willis was struck by the notion that there was one set of hands missing. Eva should've been in on this. She wasn't a member of the family but she was becoming important to him and to the children. And that scared him. He'd never felt this way about any woman, not even the one who hurt him the most.

Chapter Nine

Eva was disappointed when Willis didn't accompany the children to her home the next morning. Harley came in and handed her the enrollment forms she had been asking Willis to provide. She took them happily. Harley sat with them for a while, but he soon excused himself. He stopped before he went out the door. "I will be over at the Arnett farm today if you need me."

"*Danki*, Harley. Has your brother written to your old school asking them to send your records here?"

"I don't think so. Can't you do it?"

"I reckon I had better if I'm to get them before the start of classes." It was a simple thing she could do to help Willis.

"I will need your former teacher's name and the school address. Do you know it?"

"Sure." He supplied the information and she wrote it down.

"Where is Willis today?" She tried not to sound too curious about him.

"He's gone to a farm sale hoping to pick up some

scrap metal and another anvil. He said he would be home by five o'clock."

So she wouldn't see him until later. Hiding her disappointment Eva stared at the two children watching her. Maddie was all smiles. The dour look on Otto's face didn't bode well for the day. "Otto, I will have you start by sweeping out the classroom and making sure all the desks are clean and lined up. Maddie, I'm going to need you to help me make cookies."

"Will they be snickerdoodles?"

"I think I have the ingredients for some. Otto, what kind of cookie do you like?" She needed to engage with the boy on some level. If she couldn't break through his barrier of resistance the school year was going to be difficult.

"Oatmeal chocolate chip," he muttered.

"Two of my favorites mixed together. Good choice. The broom and dust rags are in the coat closet at the school. I'll be over later if you need any help."

His eyes snapped with anger. "I'm not so dumb that I need help sweeping the floor."

"Of course, you aren't. That isn't what I said and certainly not what I meant."

He stomped out of the house without looking back, letting the screen door slam behind him.

Maddie shook her head. "He hates it when people treat him like he's slow."

"I wasn't trying to hurt his feelings. I was only offering to help."

"I know. *Daed* used to say Otto had a chip on his shoulder and that's why he gets mad but I never see one."

Why was the boy so prickly? She didn't know and

she wasn't sure how to find out. She could only hope things improved before he started school.

Eva was finishing up in her kitchen after making a batch of blackberry jam from the bush out back when she saw a white car turn into her drive. Two women got out. They turned out to be the county social worker and a public health nurse. They left Eva papers showing what they suggested should be taught regarding health and science and gave her a schedule for vision and hearing tests in October. Working with local health and welfare people was another part of her teaching position she hadn't given much thought about. She would have to visit with the school board and learn how much of what the outsiders offered the community would accept.

They left after a brief visit and Eva was about to go across to the school when a second car pulled into her drive. This time an Amish fellow got out. She couldn't see his face but there was something familiar about him. He pulled a suitcase out of the trunk. When he turned to look at her she gave a squeal of delight and raced out the door and flew to hug him. "Danny. What are you doing here? Oh, it's so good to see you."

"It's good to see you, too, Eva." He turned to inspect the school. "So this is where you'll be spending your days."

"*Ja*, isn't it lovely? It's brand-new and so is the house. In a few days the community is holding a frolic to add a barn and corrals. I can hardly believe how fortunate I am to have landed here. How long are you staying?"

"A week or so, I think. Gene wanted to make sure you were getting along up here since the only thing you have written us about is the need for your books."

She laughed "If I wrote about everything that has

happened since I arrived in New Covenant, I would have my own book to be published."

His eyebrows shot up. "I like a good story. Maybe you should fill me in."

She took his arm and led him toward the house. "Come into my lovely little house and I will make us both some *kaffi*. I must warn you I have company. The children from across the street are staying with me during the day. Harley is thirteen, Otto is eleven and Maddie is six. I should warn you that Maddie has an imaginary friend named Bubble so please be kind to her."

"When have you known me to be anything else?"

"Never. That makes me wonder how you inherited all the kindness in the family and Gene inherited all the sour. How is he? I never thought I would say this but I have missed him and his grumpy looks. I even miss Corinne and her litany of aches and pains."

"Gene is fine, but some things have changed. I'll tell you about it over that coffee."

Eva held open the screen door. A single bark alerted her to the fact that Sadie was on her way to make a visit. She glanced inside the house and saw Maddie coloring at the kitchen table. "Maddie, Sadie is coming."

Maddie's eyes grew wide with joy. "She is? Can I go outside and play with her?"

"You may go outside and play with her but don't stray from the yard."

Maddie stopped in the doorway when she saw Danny standing behind Eva. "Who are you?"

Eva held a hand toward her brother. "Maddie, this is my brother Danny who has come for a visit."

"I'm Maddie Gingrich and this is my friend Bubble."

Maddie put an arm over the shoulder of her imaginary friend.

Eva waited eagerly for Danny's reaction. He glanced at her and then took his hat off. "Pleased to meet you, Maddie and Bubble."

Maddie grinned. "We're going to go play with Sadie. She kept the bear from eating us."

His eyebrows shot up. "Did you say a bear?"

"*Ja*. Come on, Bubble." Maddie raced down the steps of Eva's porch and out to see Sadie. The dog held a thick stick in her mouth. She gave it to Maddie who promptly threw it for the happy retriever.

"The bear was imaginary, too, right?" Danny asked.

Eva covered her mouth with her hand and giggled as she shook her head. "*Nee*, it was quite real. Come in and sit down. I'll tell you the whole tale while I brew you some stout *kaffi*."

After she had a pot fixed for the two of them and while it perked she recounted her adventures in New Covenant.

"All this took place in a week?" He shook his head in disbelief.

"I dread to think what the next month will bring."

"I hope you don't find yourself with a bear in the classroom."

"Fortunately, Sadie comes to the school with the children so I don't think we'll have a problem."

Eva poured them both coffee when it was finished and spread her fresh jam on several pieces of homemade bread. She sat across from her brother, took a sip from her mug and then put it down. "So. Why are you really here, Danny? It's only a little over a week since I left."

"Gene thought perhaps you would be ready to return by now."

"Oh, he did? He has very little confidence in me. So I assume he sent you to escort me home, is that it?"

Danny leaned back in his chair and ran his fingers through his thick black hair. "In a manner of speaking, but that's not why I came."

She leaned back with her arms crossed over her chest. "Do tell."

"I wanted to see for myself if you were happy here. Are you?"

Eva heard footsteps on her porch. She looked out and saw Willis in the doorway. A jolt of happiness sent her pulse racing. She smiled at Willis. "*Ja*, Danny, I am happy here. Come in, Willis. I have fresh coffee and some jam to send home with you. This is my brother Danny who surprised me with an unannounced visit."

Willis stepped inside, and the two men nodded to each other. "We are blessed to have your sister as our new teacher. I won't interrupt your reunion. I'm home from my errand. I'll take the *kinder* off your hands. Thanks for watching them. I see Maddie playing with Sadie. Where is Otto?"

"He's doing some cleaning for me inside the school."

"Has he been trouble for you?"

"Not a bit." She grabbed an unopened jar of jam and pressed it into his hands. "For you and the *kinder* to enjoy."

Willis shot a glance at her brother and mumbled his thanks. He walked to the edge of the porch and shouted for Maddie and Otto. Maddie came running with Sadie beside her. A few moments later Otto appeared at the schoolhouse door. Willis gestured for him to come on.

Otto sauntered down the steps, crossed the lawn and paused in front of his brother.

Willis smiled at the boy. "I brought pizza from town for our lunch. How does that sound?"

Maddie jumped up and down. "Yea, I love pizza. Let's go."

Willis tipped his hat toward Eva. "Thanks again."

Otto shifted his weight from one foot to the other and folded his arms tightly over his chest. "I think Teacher will want to check my work before I leave."

She shook her head. "Nope. If you did your best, then I can't ask for anything more."

He seemed surprised by her answer but didn't say anything. He took off running to catch up with Willis and Maddie. Eva waited hoping Willis would look back. He did. She waved and called out, "See you tomorrow."

He lifted his hand in a brief salute. She was still grinning as she turned back to Danny. "Where were we?"

"You were telling me that you're happy here. I can see that for myself. It didn't take you long to meet the neighbor. Seems like a nice guy."

"He is. The children are his half brothers and sister. He took them in after their parents died. It hasn't been an easy adjustment for him or for the children. I've been doing what I can to help him. As a good neighbor."

"As a neighbor. I see." Danny's grin widened with the hint of humor in his voice.

She wasn't sure what he thought was funny. "Not to change the subject but why are you here?"

"I hate to be the bearer of bad news but Corinne's mother suffered a stroke two days after you left."

"I'm sorry to hear that." Unlike Corinne, her mother was a kind and hardworking woman.

"She's still in the hospital and very weak. The doctors say she'll need a lot rehabilitation, but she should be able to come home at some point. Unfortunately, she has lost the use of her right side. Her husband isn't going to be able to take care of her alone. Corinne wants them to move into the *daadihaus* on our farm."

"That should make it much easier for Corinne to help."

"Well, that's the rub. Corinne doesn't feel she can do it by herself. Gene agrees."

Comprehension dawned and Eva's heart sank. "He wants me to come home and take care of her parents. That's why he sent you."

Eva turned away and walked to the end of the porch. She wanted to pound her hands on the railing. Her family needed her again, but she had already accepted the teaching job. She didn't want to leave New Covenant. She was making friends here even if one of them was imaginary. She bit down on her thumbnail as she wrestled with her conscience. What should she do?

"You don't have to make a decision today."

"Gene knows I want to do this. Why can't he get help from someone else in our family or from Corrine's?"

"Eva, you are under no obligation to return home. I think it's time Corinne stepped up and took care of them. They are her parents."

"But I'm the one with the most experience caring for the elderly." It was true. She'd had many years of practice. She could already visualize the things that would be needed.

"I don't know what to say. I know I should return but I don't feel that I can. I have made a commitment to this community. I have a house and it has been filled with furniture donated for my use. I have the loan of a horse and cart. I've even received three new *kapps* in this congregation's style. The people here have welcomed me with open arms. How can I walk out on them after everything they have done for me?"

"If you feel that strongly you should stay."

She spun around to face Danny. "Do you really think so? Is Gene adamant that I come home?" What was the right thing to do?

Danny shook his head. "He didn't insist that I bring you back."

"Yet." She supplied the missing word.

"It would be easy for me to tell you what to do, but you are going to have to decide for yourself. Either way, the woman is still in the hospital. There's no rush to make a decision. She may recover better than expected."

"But there is a rush. If I decide to leave, the school board will have to start searching for a teacher all over again. The more advance notice I can give them, the better."

She didn't want to leave. She knew exactly the kind of life that would be waiting for her at home. She would return to working in the background, caring for someone who could no longer care for themselves, reading about adventures rather than having them. If she went back to Illinois she wouldn't hear what Bubbles was up to each day. She wouldn't have a chance to help Otto or to see Willis again. The thought dragged her spirits lower. What should she do?

Danny came up behind her and placed his hands on her shoulders. "Don't worry about it, Eva. I am here simply to visit my sister and have her show me around the wild woods of Maine. Are there really bears?"

He dismissed her decision so easily. If only she could

do the same. "There are and also moose. I haven't seen a moose yet, but I understand they are plentiful and can be as dangerous as a bear. If you go hiking in the woods, take bear repellent and give moose a wide berth."

"Listen to you with your backwoods lore. I will tell you one thing, Eva, I have missed your cooking. Corinne's cooking is passable. That's the kindest thing I can say about it."

"If you can't say something nice it's best not to say anything."

He chuckled. "Words of advice that Corinne never took to heart. She thinks you moved away simply to make things more difficult for her."

Eva stared at him, aghast. "Did she say that?"

"She has. More than once."

"Well, perhaps I did hope that she would take on more responsibility around the house if I wasn't there."

"Gene spoiled her at your expense. You deserve a life of your own. How many times have I told you that?"

"Often enough." She glanced across the street at the Gingrich home. "Now that I have had a taste of it, I'm not sure I can give it up."

"I like Eva a lot, don't you, Willis?" Maddie was pulling the pepperoni slices from her pizza and stacking them on the edge of her plate for Bubble. One by one, she slipped them over the edge of the table to Sadie who was lying under her chair.

"Sure, I like her."

"Bubble says if you ask her to marry you she'll say yes. I wish she could eat with us. Can I go invite her?"

"Not today. She wants to visit with her brother. What did she say his name was?" He ignored the suggestion that he should marry Eva. She wouldn't have him even if he asked. She would want a smart husband. One who used fine words and read books.

"Her brother's name is Danny. He's nice, too. I think Sadie would like more pizza."

"Sadie has had enough. Did Eva's brother say why he was here?" It seemed odd that a family member would visit when she had been here less than two weeks. It made him wonder if something was wrong back home. He didn't want to come out and ask. He was used to minding his own business. Until Eva had arrived in New Covenant, he'd seldom given his neighbors a second thought.

Now he found it impossible to stop thinking about her. She had somehow wormed her way past the defenses he kept around his heart. He cared for Eva a great deal.

Maddie took back one slice of pepperoni and ate it. "Why do people get married?"

"Because they love each other, I reckon."

"What if someone matchmakes them together? Will they love each other then?"

He was sorry she'd ever heard the term. "A matchmaker is just a person who introduces two people in the hopes that they will fall in love. I don't think it works out all that often."

Maddie sighed. "I hope it works out for you."

Otto nudged Maddie. "You talk too much."

"I don't. I talk just enough."

Willis realized something was going on between the two of them. "What do you want to work out for me?"

"Nothing," Otto said quickly. He scowled at his sister.

Willis glanced between them. "I don't think *nothing* is the right word. What's going on?"

"We gave Eva a list of things we want your wife to have," Maddie said proudly.

Harley rolled his eyes. "Girls can't keep a secret."

Maddie stuck out her lower lip. "Nobody said it was a secret."

"It's not anymore." Otto got up and left the table, carrying a piece of pizza outside.

Willis shook his head. "I'm not going to find a wife, so it doesn't matter what you and Otto told Eva I needed."

"Okay." Maddie gave Sadie her last piece of pepperoni. "I'm done. Can I go out and play now?"

"It will be time for bed soon. Don't forget. Harley is going to read us a story tonight. Send Sadie home."

"Okay."

Harley cleared the table without being asked. Willis washed what few dishes there were. When the kitchen was clean, Willis sat down in his chair by the window. Maddie climbed onto his lap while Otto and Harley sprawled on the floor. Harley turned the pages of a book and stopped when he found what he was looking for. "This is the story *Mamm* liked to read to us. It's about Joseph and his brothers."

Willis knew the tale, but he listened to Harley read it with a new appreciation. No matter what he made in his forge it couldn't convey the message of God's love and the power of forgiveness as clearly as the words in Harley's book did. Eva understood that.

After the children were in bed Willis finished a set of horseshoes for his draft horses at his forge. When he was done, he stepped out into the cool night air, relieved to leave his hot workplace. The moon wasn't up yet, but the sky was littered with millions of brilliant stars. His gaze was drawn to Eva's house. The light in her sitting room was on. She was still up. He was tempted to walk over and visit for a while but stopped himself before he made such a foolish mistake.

Eva's light went out as he watched. Maybe it was her brother who was restless. And what business did he have spying on her even from a distance? He was about to turn away when he saw her front door open. She came out onto the porch, drew a shawl around her shoulders and started across the lawn to the school. She didn't go inside the building; instead, she passed behind it.

Curiosity got the better of him. Where was the new teacher going this time of night? Although there hadn't been any reports of bears in the area since Maddie's adventure, it wasn't particularly safe to be wandering alone in the dark. It was still wild country. Potato farms and towns covered the floor of the valley, but the hills on either side were timber. He started walking in that direction just to make sure she got safely to wherever she was going.

When he came around the corner of the school building, he saw her sitting on the playground swings. She pushed off and began to move back and forth.

She was safe enough where she was. He should go home, but he didn't move. Why was she out here? Was something troubling her? Drawn to her almost against his will, he crossed the lawn and approached the swings.

"Good evening, Willis. Isn't it a beautiful night?" She had seen him coming. She must have eyes like a cat.

"I reckon you're right. It's a downright pretty night."

The thick trees kept the lights from the nearby town blocked. Overhead the Milky Way stretched like a glittering gauze scarf thrown down on the floor of heaven. Across the night sky the constellations looked so close a man could almost reach out and touch them. A soft breeze brought the ever-present scent of pine to him, and underneath that the odor of the potato plants that covered much of the valley.

"What are you doing out here?" he asked.

"I'm practicing how to swing." She leaned back and pumped her legs to gain height.

He chuckled as he leaned against the A-frame metal crossbar. "I didn't know swinging required practice. I thought it was like riding a bicycle. Once you learned you never forgot."

"That might be true for you, but I need to practice. I may want to impress the children with my skills."

"Somehow, I don't think that's the whole truth. I suspect you are out here because you have something on your mind."

She gave a big sigh and leaned back as far as she could. "Mr. Gingrich, you are every bit as perceptive as Bubble."

"I'm not sure if I should take that as a compliment or not." He moved to sit in the swing beside her.

"That was meant as a compliment. I do have something on my mind."

"Does it have to do with a list?"

She frowned. "A list? *Nee*. Oh, you mean the list the children gave me. I almost forgot about it. I'm surprised they told you."

"Maddie isn't good at keeping secrets. What is contained in this list?"

"I have kept it in my pocket to share with you if you'd care to read it?" she offered.

"It's too dark. Tell me what they said."

"It's a well-thought-out list of requirements for your wife-to-be."

"From Otto and Maddie? I can't wait to hear it."

"Oh, Harley added one requirement. She should be pretty."

"At least Harley has my best interest at heart. What else?"

"She has to smell nice, be a good cook and not make them take a lot of baths."

He chuckled. "That last requirement came from Otto, didn't it?"

"It did. Oh, and she shouldn't be old but fifty like me is acceptable."

"Ouch, that had to hurt."

"They are such amazing children. I haven't been bored for a minute since I met them." She sighed deeply and fell silent.

"You said you had something on your mind. Would it help to talk about it? I can listen and swing at the same time."

She giggled. "I knew you were a man of many talents when I first laid eyes on you. Next, you will tell me you can walk and chew gum."

"I've been able to do it for years. What's troubling you, Teacher? Tell ole *Onkel* Willis."

She stopped swinging and sat still. "I have a decision to make."

He waited but she didn't say anything else. He began turning himself around until the chains were tightened. When he picked his feet up he whirled rapidly as the chains unwound.

"Don't you want to know what decision I have to make?" she asked.

"Only if you want to tell me."

"Do you know what I did before I came here?"

"I know you didn't teach school. You told me this was your first teaching job. If you want me to guess, I'll start with the A's. Were you an arrow maker?"

He heard her soft chuckle. "I lived with my brother and his wife and I took care of my grandparents. Grandmother was very frail. She was bedridden for most of the last five years."

"She was blessed to have a granddaughter willing to care for her."

"That's what everyone said. 'Isn't it wonderful that Gene and Corrine have Eva to take care of the old folks? She is such a blessing to them. What would they do without her?' When my grandparents passed away I suddenly found myself without a purpose. Do you know what that feels like?"

"I never gave it much thought. I believed my purpose was to beat hot iron into useful things."

"And a fine purpose that is."

"Is that what's troubling you? That you don't have a purpose now? What about teaching?"

"My sister-in-law's mother has had a stroke and she is going to need someone to take care of her. My brother and his wife want me to return to Illinois and be that someone."

"I see. Will you go?"

"I want to stay and teach school. Is that being selfish?"

"What if I said that I want you to stay?"

Chapter Ten

Eva turned to stare at Willis with her heart thudding rapidly. What was he implying? That he cared for her? Or was she reading something into his statement that he didn't mean? They had only known each other a little more than a week although it felt as if she had known him longer. She wished she had gone out on more dates. Nothing she had read in her books prepared her for a moonlight conversation with a man she was beginning to care for.

"What I mean is that my brothers and sister like you and they would be upset if you left." Willis ran his words together so quickly she almost laughed. "Particularly Maddie," he added.

It was foolish to think he might have meant something else. He'd made it plain from the start that he wasn't interested in dating or marriage.

"I would miss all of you terribly if I went back to Illinois."

"Then don't go."

"Isn't it my duty to return and do as my older brother wishes? He has taken the place of my father who died when I was fifteen. I lived in his household until I came here."

"Then go back and be miserable."

"What a terrible thing to say. What makes you think I'll be miserable?"

He stood up and let the swing undulate on its own. "Because you sound like it will make you miserable to return. If your brother has truly replaced your father in your life, then he will understand that at some point you need to leave the nest. I see that you have two choices. Sit on your brother's roost and squawk about your difficulties like a chicken or take off like a dove and look for your own nesting ground. Good night, Eva."

She watched him walk away. "Good night, Willis. You've been extremely unhelpful."

"That's what friends are for," he shot back.

She smiled as she watched him cross the road and enter his home. A man she could talk to without even mentioning books. Willis was a rare fellow indeed. He was turning out to be the best friend she had never had.

She would cherish that friendship and keep her girlish emotions in check. He didn't want a romantic relationship. Nor did she. Letting him suspect she felt otherwise might destroy their wonderful camaraderie.

Maddie appeared at Eva's door the next morning just before six o'clock. She cupped her hands around her eyes and pressed her face to the screen door. "Hello? Is anybody home?"

Eva walked out of the kitchen. "My, you are here early."

"Willis is fixing oatmeal for breakfast. Bubble doesn't like oatmeal so we came to see what you're having."

"I was about to fix some French toast. How does that sound?"

"Yummy."

Danny strolled to the entryway and held open the door. "I have got to get me one of those."

Maddie tipped her head to the side. "You want a bowl of oatmeal?"

"I want an imaginary friend who will check out what everyone is having for breakfast and take me to the best house."

Maddie shook her head. "Bubble didn't check with everybody. Just Willis and Eva."

Eva chuckled. "I love to cook for my friends. Real and imaginary. Go wash your hands, Maddie, and breakfast will be ready in a few minutes."

"I have to do something first." Maddie raced out the door toward her home.

"I don't believe I've ever met anyone quite like that child." Danny poured himself a cup of coffee from the percolator on the stove and sat at the table.

"I don't believe there is anyone quite like Maddie anywhere," Eva said as she began cracking eggs.

"You were out late last night." Danny cast a glance at her over the top of his mug.

"Was I? I guess I didn't notice what time it was."

"If it was me coming in that late you would be right in thinking I was out with a girl."

"What are you suggesting, brother dear?"

"I'm not suggesting anything because I have known you to burn the pancakes of someone who's getting on your nerves. I assume the same applies to French toast."

"It's amazing how well you understand me. Gene was never able to put two and two together."

"He ate a lot of blackened pancakes over the years. I take it that you've made up your mind."

She smiled at him. "I wish I could say that I have. I'm praying about it."

"*Wunderbar.* Now I can enjoy a few carefree days with my sister. Will you show me around your school this morning?"

"I'd be delighted to do that. We can go over after breakfast." She began whipping her eggs. "I wonder what's keeping Maddie?"

"I'll take a look." He stood and stepped out onto the porch. "You might want to put a few more eggs in that bowl. I hope you have enough bread."

"What are you talking about?"

He stepped aside and held open the door as Maddie came in followed by Willis, Otto and Harley.

"What did you need to see me about?" Willis asked, worry creasing his brow.

Eva fisted her hands on her hips and leaned down to address Maddie. "What do you think you are doing, young lady?"

"No one in my family likes oatmeal, so Bubble invited them over here to have breakfast with you."

Willis looked confused. Eva didn't blame him. He scowled at his sister. "You said Eva needed to see me right away."

Eva straightened. "Well now that you're all here you might as well stay. Please have a seat. Boys, there are extra chairs in my sitting room. Go ahead and bring them in here."

Maddie climbed into the chair she liked best. It was the one next to where Eva normally sat. Otto sniffed the air near the stove. "That sure smells a lot better than oatmeal."

Willis glared at Eva as he pulled his hat from his head. "You shouldn't let her get away with this. One of these days her tall tales are going to get her in more trouble than she can handle."

"You're right of course, but I find her too charming to scold."

His eyes narrowed. "You're going to make me be the stern one, aren't you?"

"Indeed I am. That's what friends are for."

"I knew I'd regret that crack," he muttered. He sat on a chair and lifted Maddie to his lap. "You can't make things like this up, Maddie. Have you heard the story of the boy who cried wolf?"

She fastened her gaze on her bare toes. "Maybe."

"We've all heard it," Harley said. "It was one of *Daed*'s favorite lessons."

"It means if you tell a fib often enough people will stop believing you when you need them to listen to the truth."

Maddie raised her head and started to say something but Willis cut her off. "You can't blame this on Bubble."

Her shoulders slumped. "Okay. I'm sorry I said Eva needed to see you right away."

"I was frightened that something was wrong. You are forgiven but don't forget what I've said."

She looked at him from beneath her lashes. "But I'm not sorry we're going to have French toast for breakfast."

"Neither am I," Otto chimed in.

"Then enjoy the treat today because it will be oatmeal again tomorrow and no complaining. Understood?"

"Understood," they all replied.

He put Maddie down and looked at Danny. "My advice is to avoid having kids until your hair is already starting to turn gray because they surely speed the process."

Danny chuckled. "Good advice."

"What do you do back in Illinois?" Willis stepped to the cupboard and brought out more plates. He handed them to the boys and Maddie.

"I'm a cabinetmaker by trade. I work in a factory with about thirty other Amish fellows. I also farm with my brother."

"Is the factory Amish owned?" Willis asked.

"It's not. An *Englisch* company owns several plants across the state. We make everything from kitchen cabinets to dressers and nightstands. The *Englisch* like tacking on a label that says 'Amish Made.' They can push up the price that way."

"Danny is a supervisor in the plant near our home. He has done well for himself." Eva couldn't keep a touch of pride from creeping into her voice.

"We could use a good tradesman up here if you get tired of working for the *Englisch*. Our bishop owns a backyard shed-building business, but he is branching out into building tiny homes. I understand they are all the rage."

"I've heard that. I wish him success, but I can't see moving here to do the same thing I do back home only for less money."

"Money isn't everything," Eva said, wondering why she hadn't thought to ask Danny to stay. It would be wonderful to have him close by.

"It can buy happiness," Maddie said with a grin.

"Money *can't* buy happiness," Otto said, shaking his head at her mistake.

"Well, if there was a puppy named Happiness, money could buy her." Maddie stuck her tongue out at her brother.

"That's not the same thing," Otto snapped.

Maddie crossed her arms and glared at him. "If I had money I'd buy you some happiness 'cause you're grumpy all the time."

"Children, be nice to each other," Willis cautioned, "or I will take you home before Eva puts food on your plates."

"Sorry, Otto." Maddie's overly contrite expression made Eva choke on a laugh.

"Me, too," Otto added, but he didn't bother trying to sound sincere.

"Put some happiness in Otto's food, please, Eva," Maddie said in a tiny voice sweeter than the maple syrup she was pouring over her toast.

Eva saw Willis struggling not to laugh. She covered her mouth with her hands in an attempt to stay quiet but lost the battle as soon as her eyes met his. A second later everyone was laughing.

Willis couldn't remember a time when he had enjoyed a meal more. Eva was unfazed by the arrival of four hungry guests first thing in the morning. She turned out piece after piece of golden-brown French toast with a smile and some funny comment. Willis even liked her brother. He was an unassuming fellow with the same honey-brown hair and gray-green eyes. It was how a family meal should feel.

Maddie enjoyed being the center of attention. She

didn't mention her friend Bubble for the entire meal. Even Otto and Harley seemed to come out of their shells when Danny started discussing baseball. He occasionally attended a Chicago Cubs game and was able to discuss batting averages and the Cub's up-and-coming pitchers with the boys. Harley followed the Cubs in the newspapers and on the radio when he was able to listen to a game. The local feed store back in Maryland broadcast baseball games over their sound system for their Amish customers and in the process sold more feed.

"What are your plans for today?" Eva asked him.

"The same thing I have planned every day. Take a piece of iron, get it real hot and then bang on it until it looks like something."

"Don't let him fool you," Eva said to her brother. "He's very skilled at what he does."

"What will you do with my siblings while I'm working?" Willis asked.

"I have plenty to keep me busy at the school. I'm making folders for each of my scholars in case I need a substitute teacher for any reason. That way another teacher can quickly see each child's strengths or challenges. I was hoping that Maddie could give me a hand."

"Will I get to color again?" Maddie asked.

"Absolutely," Eva replied. "I have colored chalk you can use on the blackboard."

"*Danki.* Can we go now?"

Willis shook his head. "No one goes anywhere until the dishes are done. Eva was kind enough to cook for us. The least we can do is clean up after ourselves."

Eva gave him a sweetly grateful look. It made him realize how much more he would like to do for her. A little voice in the back of his mind told him he was becoming too attached to her, but he ignored it for now.

It only took a few minutes to get the plates washed and put away. Although Willis had work to do he tagged along as they walked to the school to hear what Danny had to say.

The first thing Eva's brother noticed was the boarded-up window. "What happened here?"

"Otto broke it," Maddie said, earning a sour look from her older brother.

Willis could tell that Otto was embarrassed, but he chose to own up to what he had done. "I hit a rock through it."

"Line drive or high fly foul ball?" Danny was trying to look serious.

"Line drive," Otto said quietly.

"On purpose or was it an accident?"

"It was sort of an accident." Otto looked up to judge Danny's reaction.

"How much did that set you back?"

"Enough. Your sister said I have to work after school for two months."

"The time will go by quickly enough."

"Danny is an expert on broken windows," Eva said, a sly grin curving her pretty lips.

"That was a long time ago, Eva." A wave of red crept up Danny's neck.

"He and some friends broke four windows in Arthur, Illinois, one night."

"Four? This many?" Maddie held up the correct number of fingers. "Did you get in trouble for that?"

"Lots and lots of trouble," Danny admitted.

Otto looked impressed. Willis thought he saw a gleam of hero worship in his young brother's eyes.

Danny must've noticed it, too. "Three of my friends came up with the idea to scare a couple of bully boys who picked on us whenever they could. They were older and they ran with a tough crowd. We didn't mean any harm but one of the rocks hit a boy in the head. He ended up in the hospital and almost lost the sight in one eye. It turned out okay, but that was the last time I followed a stupid suggestion from one of my friends. Now I think of the consequences before I act. God gave us a conscience for good reason. I would've saved everyone a lot of grief if I had listened to it back then."

Willis could see Otto mulling over Danny's comment. If even a little of it sank into the boy's head, Willis would be grateful to Eva's brother. Willis caught Eva's eye and she winked. It was exactly why she had wanted him to tell the story.

Inside the school, Eva happily showed off her desk, the supplies that had been donated and the chair that had upended her dignity the first day she arrived. Willis hung back near the outside door. Danny took a closer look at the cabinetry. He opened and closed the doors and drawers and gave Willis a thumbs-up sign. "Someone put a lot of care into this work. It should last a long time. I really like the heavy hinges and the big cabinet pulls. Are they your work, Willis?"

"Jesse Crump and Bishop Schultz made the cabinets. I did all the hardware."

"From scratch?"

"That's what I do. I hammer on a piece of hot metal until it makes something."

"Do you sell these?"

"If someone orders a set, sure."

"Do you have a few lying around?"

"I don't but I will be happy to make you some."

"Go ahead and make me a sample of a dozen different styles. I know someone who might be interested in purchasing them in bulk."

"I don't make things in bulk. I make them one at a time. Each one is a little different."

"As the owner of the company I work for would say, that's the charm of an object handmade by Amish craftsmen."

"This Amish blacksmith should get back to work," Willis said. "The potato harvest will start in a few weeks and everyone needs some sort of part made or repaired for their old potato digger. They don't appreciate the charm of my work, only that I get it done as quick as possible."

Harley, who was standing by the windows, turned to look outside. "The Fisher family is here. Do you want to get your hands dirty, Danny?"

"What do you have in mind?" Danny crossed the windows to look out. Willis followed him. Ezekiel Fisher and his four sons had rolled up in a large wagon pulled by a pair of gray draft horses.

"They are going to dig and pour the foundation for the new barn," Willis said.

"Mr. Fisher looks like he has plenty of help. If those are his sons, they are a strapping bunch. Are those two twins?"

"Triplets." Willis grinned at Danny's surprised expression. "Asher, Gabriel and Seth. Moses is the youngest. They are wheelwrights and buggy makers. The Lord has blessed us. Our community is growing rapidly."

Danny grinned. "The Lord has certainly blessed that father. I'll be happy to lend a hand today. All I need is a shovel and a pair of gloves."

"I can get that for you," Otto said.

When Otto, Harley and Danny went out the door Maddie followed them and Willis turned his attention to Eva. "I like your brother."

"I like him, too. He's a lot different than my older brother."

"So have you made your decision?" He prayed for her to stay but he wanted her to be content wherever she went.

She shook her head. "I haven't. I want to stay here. I want to become a fixture in the community of New Covenant. I had hoped to grow old and gray and have my students come back and visit me for years after they've graduated to tell me what a wonderful impact I made on their lives."

"So why not stay?"

"I'm trying to figure out *Gott*'s plan for me. I'm praying He will show me the answer I need soon."

It was hard not to admit how happy he would be if she stayed and how sad he would be if she left. "I hate the idea of losing a *goot* neighbor."

Eva chuckled. "Are you afraid the next teacher might complain about your hammering at all hours of the day and night?"

"It's rare that I work at night."

"Then she'll complain about your noisemaking while her scholars are trying to study but she still might make you some blackberry jam."

"What faults do you have that I can complain about?"

"Ha. That's a trick question if I've ever heard one. If

you haven't noticed my faults, I'm certainly not going to point them out to you."

He cupped one hand over his chin. "I'll have to study on that for a while. I'm sure you have them."

"And it would be un-Christian of you to point them out. Speaking of, I know this coming Sunday is our prayer meeting, but I haven't heard where it's going to be held."

"I believe the Fishers are hosting this time."

"I hope the weather stays fine."

"If it is raining, I will take you up in my buggy."

She inclined her head, and the ribbons of her *kapp* fell forward. "Why, thank you, neighbor Willis. That's very generous."

"I didn't say for free. I will expect two jars of jam as payment."

She laughed. "One jar of jam and one loaf of fresh bread."

"It's a deal." He realized he was smiling foolishly but he didn't care.

She opened her desk drawer and pulled out a stack of papers. She looked up at him. "Don't you have to go to work?"

He did, but he didn't want to leave. It was too much fun to spend time teasing her and laughing with her. Neighbors until they were both old and gray. It didn't sound bad.

But would he be able to keep his secret from her for years or would she discover how dimwitted he really was? And then what would she think of him?

Chapter Eleven

Eva saw the smile on Willis's face fade and wondered why. Was he unhappy that she might be leaving New Covenant? Maybe she assumed he was thinking about her when he had something else on his mind.

"What's wrong, Willis?"

"Nothing. I was thinking about what your brother said. That he knows someone who might buy hardware from me.

"Do you think they will purchase some of your work?"

"I think it's worth a try to find out."

"When could you have enough pieces ready to show them?"

"Two weeks maybe."

"That's exciting. Why aren't you smiling?"

He did smile at her then. "It's a pretty big *if*."

Her heart grew lighter once more. "I think when the Good Lord inspires us we should hold on to that hope."

After Willis left the schoolhouse she went to work on making folders for each student where she could keep their information handy. That way, another teacher could quickly read up on each scholar. Once the folders were finished, Eva found herself struggling to concentrate on her lesson plan for the first week of school. More and more, her thoughts were drawn to Willis. His brothers and sister were delightful, but Willis had a stronger hold on her emotions. As much as she wanted to rationalize it away, it wasn't working. She was falling for her friend. If he didn't return her feelings then staying in New Covenant would become much more difficult.

She got up and went to check on Maddie. The little girl was busy building mud pies and cookies. Otto, Harley and Danny were helping the Fisher brothers string chalk lines in a large rectangle to make sure the building would be straight and square. Maddie got up from her play kitchen and carried several pies on a piece of bark to the Fishers. They each stopped what they were doing and made a production out of sampling her offering. They were too old to be Eva's students but none of them appeared to be married as they were all clean-shaven. Maddie was doing her best to impress them with her pie-making skills.

Eva was ready for a break by midmorning. She went back to her house to fix some lunch for herself and the Gingrich kids. She was dicing celery for chicken salad when Constance Schultz and Dinah Lapp stopped in.

"I had to see how you were getting along," Constance said as she came in.

"I'm fine. Just anxious for school to start. Everything seems to be in place. The only things I don't have are my library books but I should get them any day."

"*Goot.* I see they are working on the barn foundation. You were told we are having a frolic to raise it on Monday, right?"

"*Ja*, I heard."

"I also came to let you know we have another new family that arrived a few days ago. A young widow, her father-in-law and her daughter. She is the granddaughter of Samuel Yoder. He convinced them to settle here. Her name is Becca Beachy. I believe the child will be in the first grade. They purchased the old Kent farm on Pendleton Road."

Dinah made a sour face. "That house hasn't been lived in for years."

Constance nodded. "That's why I intend to organize a frolic for tomorrow. With all of us working we can get the house in shipshape in no time. We are spreading the word and you may do so, as well, Eva. So far Bethany, Gemma, Penelope Martin, myself and Dinah are going."

It was her first opportunity to join the women of the New Covenant congregation in a charitable endeavor and she was pleased to be asked. Taking care of each other was as important to the Amish as taking care of family members. Eva was beginning to feel she truly belonged among these North Country Amish and she gave thanks for the many gifts the Lord had given her since she arrived. Especially for the friendship Willis had extended to her. If only she could be sure she would be staying.

Bright and early the next morning, Constance turned her buggy into the schoolyard. Eva and Maddie had been waiting for her and hurried out with a basket of supplies. "Does the family know we are coming?"

"*Nee*, I thought we would make it a surprise."

The shocked expression on Becca Beachy's face when she opened the door proved Constance right. The women all introduced themselves. Dinah gestured to Eva. "This will be your daughter's teacher when school starts."

Becca, a soft-spoken woman in her early twenties with dark hair and dark eyes extended her hand to Eva. "My daughter is looking forward to school." She smiled at Maddie who was uncharacteristically quiet. "I hope there will be other children her age attending. Will you be in school?"

Maddie didn't say a word. She had her face against Eva's skirt.

Eva patted her head. "This is Maddie Gingrich. She is also a first grader. Is your daughter here?"

Becca shook her head. "She's gone with my father-in-law to purchase some dairy cows, but they should be back soon. Please come in. I'm afraid I'm out of coffee, but I can offer you some tea."

Constance walked past Becca into the kitchen and set her basket on the table and pulled out a coffee tin. "I brought some with me. We're here to tackle the dust so let's get started, sisters."

The other women gathered around the table, each one with a basket or pail filled with cleaning supplies.

Becca pressed a hand to her cheek. "I hadn't expected this much help from the community so quickly."

Eva carried her pail to the sink and began to fill it with water. "I can start on the windows."

"I'll get this food put away," Bethany said as she opened her basket. She brought out two loaves of bread, butter and a cheese spread and finally a cherry pie with a golden lattice crust. Penelope Miller began unpacking pint jars filled with canned fruits and vegetables.

Becca shook her head. "This is overwhelming. *Danki.* I've already cleaned two bedrooms and this kitchen. If you could help me drag the mattresses outside from the other two bedrooms so I can beat the dust out of them I would appreciate it."

The house quickly became a flurry of activity as the women attacked the floors, walls and even the ceilings with pine-scented cleaner and elbow grease. Eva was amazed at how quickly the dilapidated farmhouse took on new life as grimy windows were cleaned, rubbish hauled out and the floors scrubbed and polished. Even Maddie was given the task of polishing the kitchen cabinet doors that she could reach.

The group broke for lunch at noon and decided to eat outside. Eva was shocked when Willis walked in the door with the bishop while she was fixing a plate. Willis wrinkled his nose. Eva smiled at him and chuckled. "We are about to eat outside where the scent of real pine trees isn't as overpowering as the cleaner we have been using. What are you doing here?"

Bishop Schultz smiled at her. "I asked Willis to come take a look at some machinery Mr. Beachy purchased along with this farm. He's not sure it's in working order."

Willis pushed the brim of his straw hat back with one finger. "I can usually make a part for less than what the owner would have to pay to buy one. I won't know if it's something I can fix until I get a good look at it."

"The property has been planted in potatoes and hay," the bishop added. "The church will help Mr. Beachy get his first crops harvested. I just wanted to know if we should bring our own machinery. Is your father-in-law about?" he asked Becca.

"I think that is him now." A pickup pulling a silver cattle trailer turned into the drive. An elderly Amish man who walked with a cane got out of the truck and helped a little girl out. She came running over to see her mother. "We have four cows now and *Daadi* is going to show me how to milk them."

Becca put her arm around the child. "This is my daughter, Annabeth. These nice women have come to help me clean the house and this is our new bishop. And this little girl will be in the first grade with you when school starts. Her name is Maddie."

The two girls sized each other up. Annabeth spoke first. "Do you want to come see our new cows?"

Maddie nodded and the two girls started toward the barn. "Stay away from the truck and the trailer until they have the cattle unloaded," Becca called after them.

"We will," they replied in unison.

Becca pressed a hand to her chest. "That went better than I was hoping. She hasn't had anyone her own age to play with for ages."

Willis raised both eyebrows. "I'm happy to have someone for Maddie to play with, too. She has an imaginary friend if Annabeth should mention meeting someone called Bubble."

Willis and the bishop went out to speak to Mr. Beachy.

"Tell us a little about yourself," Constance said as she handed Becca a plate with a sandwich, some grapes and wedges of cheese.

"There isn't a lot to tell. I'm from Pinecrest, Florida."

"What?" Dinah looked ready to fall over. "You moved from the beautiful beaches of Florida to the northernmost county in Maine? Are you out of your mind?"

Everyone laughed. "Pay her no attention," Constance said. "Dinah has been trying to get her husband to take her there for years."

"I lived in Pinecrest for a short time," Gemma said. "I worked at the Amish Pie Shop. Do you know it?"

"I do. Perhaps we saw each other there. My husband loved their rhubarb pie."

The sadness in her eyes told Eva it had been a love match. Eva wondered how the young husband lost his life but she didn't ask. The Amish rarely spoke of the dead or of their grief. The passing of a loved one was the will of God and not to be questioned.

Becca and Gemma began talking about people and places they both had known in Florida. The beginnings of a new friendship seemed to be flourishing between the two. Eva had been involved in frolics before, but today she felt she truly belonged in the community of New Covenant. She glanced out the kitchen window. The bishop stood beside Mr. Beachy while Willis was on his knees looking under a rusty machine. He lay down on his back and wriggled beneath it. She grinned at the sight. A wife would have trouble keeping his clothes clean. The kids should have added being a good laundress to their list.

"What are you smiling about?" Bethany asked.

Caught off guard, Eva stumbled over her reply. "Am I smiling? I reckon I'm just happy to be useful today."

Bethany tipped her head to the side. "That was more of a daydreamy smile."

Eva felt a blush heat her cheeks. She wanted to deny it but she couldn't.

"Do I detect a hint of romance in the air?" Dinah asked. All the women looked at Eva, waiting for her answer.

"*Nee*, you are mistaken." Willis's affection for her was that of a friend. If hers was something more she was the one who had to deal with that.

Dinah walked over and looked out the window. "It's Willis Gingrich, I'm guessing."

"Ah, that makes sense." Bethany nodded. "A helpful neighbor, adorable children, a strong, hardworking blacksmith. What's not to like?"

"Has the date been set?" Constance asked and everyone giggled.

Eva shook her head. "*Nee*, nothing like that. We get along well. We are friends. I look after the children for him sometimes. Don't make it out to be something that it's not."

Dinah let out a long sigh. "This means we'll be looking for another teacher soon."

"I fully intend to keep teaching for as long as the good Lord wills."

Annabeth and Maddie came in together. Annabeth tugged on her mother's sleeve. "Maddie told me a secret. Can I tell you?"

"I'm sure it involves her imaginary friend Bubble," Eva said with a smile.

Annabeth shook her head. "Maddie is getting a new mother and it's her teacher."

Everyone turned to stare at Eva. She wanted to sink into the ground. "Maddie is mistaken."

No one looked convinced.

It wasn't until Willis and Maddie came over with their plates that Eva had a chance to speak to the child. "Maddie, I'm very disappointed in you."

"What now?" Willis asked, eyeing his sister.

Eva kept her gaze on Maddie, too embarrassed to meet Willis's eyes. "You can't make up things that aren't true. Why would you tell Annabeth such a story?"

Maddie shrugged her small shoulders. "I don't know."

"I'm not going to like this, am I?" Willis asked.

"That is not an explanation, Maddie. She told Anna-beth that I was going to be her new mother. Annabeth told everyone else in the room." Eva could barely get the words out because as upset as she was with the child she was even more upset that it could never be true.

"What?" Willis looked around. "No wonder every-one is staring at us."

Maddie looked down at her feet. "I said it because you're so nice. You like me. And you remind me of my *mamm*. I started wishing it was true and then I started thinking it was true. I'm sorry."

It was hard to be angry with someone who looked so dejected. "I know you're sorry for what you did but this storytelling has to stop. You can't make something come true by wishing for it, or by making up stories about it."

Maddie started crying and it almost broke Eva's heart. Willis lifted her onto his lap. "We talked about this, Maddie. I thought you understood that it was wrong to make up stories."

"Bubble said…"

Eva shook her finger. "None of this can be blamed on Bubble. I just vehemently denied that we were in a ro-mantic relationship, which by the way every one of those women approves of, so what do we do now?"

He rubbed his knuckles on his cheek stubble. "Talk will die down eventually. I'm afraid the more we deny it the more they will think it's true. That's the way of human nature. I'm going to take her home. You will spend the rest of the day in your room, Maddie. Go get in the buggy."

The child walked away with dragging footsteps. When she reached his buggy, she glanced back but she didn't say anything. After she climbed inside, Eva pressed a hand to her heart. "She looks so sad."

"Do you think I was too tough on her?"

"I don't think so. I hope she has learned her lesson. If Samuel Yoder gets wind of this story he could say I'm not fit to teach the children."

"You don't think he would take it to heart, do you? She's just a little kid."

"Who can say."

"Well, there is one good thing about this," he said, rising to his feet with his back to the other women.

"Tell me quickly. I need to know."

"You check a couple of items off the wife-to-be wish list. You're only fifty and you're a good cook."

"Go away."

"Guess I'll see you tomorrow at church. Remember I'm happy to give you and Danny a lift if the weather is bad."

"I remember. *Danki*." She hoped it would rain and she could travel to the Fisher farm seated beside Willis. It wouldn't stop any gossip about them, but she was willing to risk a few knowing looks and awkward questions in order to spend more time with him. Such brief moments together were all she could expect, but she was rapidly growing to believe they would never be enough.

It was raining when Eva woke. She sprang from bed and hurried into her best Sunday dress. It was a deep maroon with an apron of the same color. She put up her hair and pinned her *kapp* in place. Although it was vain, she took a moment to pinch some color into her cheeks. She shook her head sadly. Was she trying to check "being pretty" off the list? That was a hopeless task.

At least Willis didn't seem to mind her appearance. Would riding to church with him fuel the gossip she was sure would circulate today? If it did, it would be a small price to pay for time spent in his company.

She had to admit she was falling for Willis, but it was a secret she would guard closely lest it ruin their friendship.

Willis pulled his buggy to stop outside her front door. She gathered together the food she had prepared for the noon meal and went to the end of the hallway. "Hurry up, Danny. Willis is here."

Her brother came out of her guest room dressed in his Sunday best. He wore a black suit coat over a vest, a white shirt and dark pants. He carried his black, flat-crowned hat in his hand. "The rain is letting up. We can take the cart."

"We will be more comfortable in Willis's buggy. It might start raining again and I have no wish to arrive at my first church service here looking like a drowned rat."

She hurried outside. Willis wore a suit almost identical to her brother's. He looked particularly handsome. She was so used to seeing him with a leather apron and rolled-up sleeves that she almost didn't recognize him. He helped her into the front seat. Maddie sat quietly in the back, wearing a pretty green dress with a white apron and a white *kapp* on her head that Eva had finished the night before last. Otto and Harley looked clean and uncomfortable in their Sunday best.

Danny climbed in the back. "Morning, Willis. Boys. Maddie, you seem quiet today. Is something wrong?"

"I got in trouble for telling someone Eva was going to be my new *mamm*."

"Which isn't true," Eva and Willis said at the same time.

"Good to know," Danny said with a smirk and a wink at his sister. She turned to stare out the windshield.

The trip to the Fisher farm was less than a mile. It started raining again, and Willis didn't hurry. What was he thinking about? Was he as happy to ride beside her as she was to be sitting beside him? Their times on the swings together made her believe he was. Good friends enjoying each other's company. If she was courting a heartache in the future she pushed that thought aside.

He leaned closer. "You smell nice. Like cinnamon and fresh bread. Have you been baking?"

"Check, check," she said, knowing it would make him laugh to refer to the list. It did.

She turned to the boys in the back. "I hope you enjoy my rolls after the service."

"What if they are all gone before we get through the line?" Otto asked.

"I kept a second pan at the house in case you wanted some for breakfast tomorrow."

Willis grinned. "You are spoiling them."

"Nonsense. I intend to teach Otto how to make them so they can enjoy them whenever they like."

"You're going to teach Otto to bake?" Harley moaned. "Argh, I'm never going to eat a cinnamon roll again."

In spite of their slow place, they soon turned into the Fisher farm. The service was to be held in the barn. Eva and Maddie took the food up to the house where Mrs. Fisher and the older women of the community were preparing to serve the meal when the preaching was done.

After visiting briefly and getting a few sidelong glances but no direct questions about her marriage plans, Eva walked into the barn. The sun had come out and shone brightly beyond the open barn doors at the other end. Rows of wooden benches had already been set up and were filled with worshippers, men on one side, women on the other, all waiting for the church service to begin. The wooden floor had been swept clean of every stray straw.

Eva and Maddie sat with the single women and girls while the married women sat up front. Glancing across the aisle to where the men sat, she caught Willis's eye. He was near the back among the single men and boys along with his brothers and Danny. He smiled at her and she smiled back shyly.

As everyone waited for the *Volsinger* to begin leading the first hymn, Eva closed her eyes. She heard the quiet rustle of fabric on wooden benches as the worshippers tried to get comfortable. The songs of the birds in the trees outside came in through the open door. The scent of alfalfa hay mingled with the smells of the animals and fresh pine as a gentle breeze swirled around her.

The song leader started the first hymn with a deep, clear voice. No musical instruments were allowed by their Amish faith. More than fifty voices took up the solemn, slow-paced cadence of the song. The ministers and the bishop were in the farmhouse across the way, agreeing on the order of the service and the preaching that would be done.

Outsiders found it strange that Amish ministers and bishops received no formal training. Instead, they were chosen by lot, accepting that God wanted them to lead the people according to His wishes. They all preached from the heart, without a written sermon. They depended on the Lord to inspire them in their readings from the Bible.

The first song came to an end. After a few minutes of silence, the *Volsinger* began the second song. It was always *Das Loblied*, the hymn of praise. When it ended, the ministers and the bishop entered the barn. As they made their way to the minister's bench, they shook hands with the men they passed.

For the next several hours Eva listened to the sermons delivered first by each of the ministers and then by the bishop interspersed with long hymns. She glanced over at Danny and Willis. Danny had his hymnbook open. Willis didn't, but he was singing. She wondered how many of the songs in the large *Ashbund* he had committed to memory. She knew only a few by heart. Maddie was surprisingly quiet.

When the three hours of preaching and singing came to an end, Bishop Schultz announced the school barn raising, and listed what supplies were still needed and then gave a final blessing. The service was over.

The scrabble of the young boys in the back making a quick getaway made a few of the elders scowl in their direction. Harley and Otto were among the first out the door. Eva grinned. She remembered how hard it was to sit still at that age. Although the young girls left with more decorum, they were every bit as anxious to be out taking advantage of the beautiful day. Winter would be upon them all too soon. She let Maddie follow them out.

Eva happened to glance at Willis again and caught him staring at her. All the other men were gone.

Gemma stopped by with her baby in her arms. "You should stop looking at that man like you are a starving mouse and he is a piece of cheese. No point in denying it."

Eva rose to her feet. "I'm not a starving mouse."

"You're doing a good impression of one." The two of them went out together and soon joined the rest of the women who were setting up the food. The elders were served first. The younger members had to wait their turn. When Willis came inside to eat, Otto and Harley were with him. He walked past Eva without a word. At first she was hurt but she soon realized they were both under an unusual amount of scrutiny. Ignoring each other was one way of putting the rumors to rest. She was thankful for his thoughtfulness. She accepted a ride home from Jesse and Gemma, leaving her brother to return with Willis and his family. She could do her part to limit the gossip as well as he could.

Later that night she took a stroll and ended up at the swing set on the school playground. It wasn't long before a lone figure stepped out of the shadows and her heart began to hammer in her chest.

Chapter Twelve

Willis walked slowly toward the swings. He had tried to talk himself out of coming tonight. Things were becoming too complicated for him. And it was all because of her. He had no idea what to do about it. He knew what he wanted; he wanted Eva in his life. Not just to give her a ride to church on a rainy morning or to spend a few stolen moments on the schoolyard swings at night. He wanted more, and he was heading for a heartbreak if he thought he could have it.

He saw her waiting for him, and his breath quickened as a surge of happiness slipped through his veins. Even though he knew he should turn around and go home he kept walking until he reached her. "Can I give you a push, Teacher?"

"That would be lovely."

She was lovely both inside and out. He knew he wasn't smart but the men in her community must've been blockheads not to have snapped her up.

He gave her a few gentle pushes before taking a seat on the swing beside her. She let her momentum slow gradually until she was stopped. "Was your day awkward?"

"I got some razzing from my friends. Jesse and Michael mostly. They are happily settled down and think I should be, too. How about you? Were there any more questions about who you are seeing?"

"Gemma was the only one who made a comment. Why can't people accept that a man and a woman can be friends without any strings attached?"

"I'm sure it happens but it's rare. Especially among us Amish. The bishop says it is the duty of men and women to marry and have children. Our people don't look for careers. God, family and community are what we value."

"At least you got it half-right. You don't have a wife but you've got three wonderful kids. I don't have anything to show for my years on this earth. I guess that's why I hope I make a good teacher."

"You will. You'll make a wonderful teacher."

"Maddie was very subdued today. She must've taken our scolding to heart."

"I noticed she didn't have much to say. Will you hate me if I say I rather enjoyed it?"

She chuckled, and he wished he could see her face. He loved the way her eyes lit up when she was excited about something. The way she chewed on her thumbnail when she was deep in thought. He was getting to know her better than most other people in his life. And he wanted to know more. He wanted to know everything about her.

"What's the best book that you read this week?" he asked, knowing she would happily chatter away about some novel or other.

"I've been reading about dyslexia and how to help little children overcome their inability to read."

"And did you learn anything new?"

"I think maybe I did. I'm going to see if I can use any of it to help Otto improve."

"What if he doesn't want to get better?"

She sighed. "Then I will consider myself a failure as a teacher."

"I don't see that. Overeager maybe but not a failure. Otto is a sensitive kid. He'll understand that you're only trying to help."

"I hope so. I can't imagine going through life without being able to read. Books aside, if you can read, you can do just about anything. With a cookbook you can create wonderful meals. You can read the weather forecast and the baseball scores in the newspaper. You can see who's having babies and what land is for sale." Her voice rose with excitement. "You can even see what's in the cat food if you're dying of curiosity and want to read the label."

"Oh, every fella needs to know what's in Tabby's treats. Imagine the horrible life Otto will have without knowing that."

She slanted him a sharp look. "Now you're making fun of me."

"Just a little. You get so passionate. You make it easy for me to get your goat. It's fun watching the steam coming out of your ears."

"If by that you mean I get angry, maybe I do a little. I know that advanced education is not necessary to our way of life. But I do believe there are students who should go on to higher learning. Samuel Yoder would have a fit if he heard me say that, wouldn't he? The bishop might have me shunned."

"I don't think so. Did you want to be one of those kids? Ones that went to high school and on to college?"

"Not really. My eighth grade education was enough because I found solace in reading. I discovered I never have to stop learning. What about you, Willis? Is there something you wanted to do but never had the chance?"

"You're going to laugh."

"I won't. I promise"

"I always wanted to learn to fly an airplane."

"Is that so? I never would've guessed that about you. You seem to me to be a man with his feet planted firmly on the ground."

"It just goes to show how well I can hide my feelings."

"That's something I'm not very good at. But I have been getting some practice lately."

He tipped his head to study her face. "What do you have to hide, Eva Coblentz?"

That I'm falling in love with you.

If she answered his question honestly, she wouldn't have anything left to hide and she might lose the friendship she cherished.

She stared at the ground. "I'm trying to hide how afraid I am that my brother and his wife will make me go back to Illinois."

"They can't really do that if you don't let them."

"When I think how hard it will be to cut myself off from them I'm not sure I can make that choice."

She could leave New Covenant when Danny went back and take up her old life. Or she could stay and try to make a satisfying life across the road from Willis

Gingrich. Neither of her choices appealed to her. She didn't want to exist on the fringe of Willis's life. That was all she had done until now. Exist. If only she could discover what he thought about her, not as a neighbor or as a friend, but as a woman.

If he gave her any kind of encouragement she was liable to throw caution to the wind and tell him exactly how much she thought of him. She was falling head over heels for the blacksmith. He had forged a band around her heart that might never be broken.

He was amazing with the children. He had a craft that he had honed to near perfection. If he could cook he would be the perfect husband. For a second she thought she had said it out loud but his expression had changed.

"So what are we going to do?" she asked.

"About what?"

"About the stories that Maddie spread about you and me?"

He shrugged. "Ride it out, I guess and hope our reputations can take the heat and make sure she understands she can't tell people we're planning to wed. I can't understand why that is important to her."

"Do you think she is afraid of being left alone again?" Eva asked.

"Maybe so. It would make sense. I'm not sure there's anything we can do to change that. When she's old enough she will have her faith to sustain her. I reckon I can reassure her that the boys and I will always take care of her and she doesn't need to be afraid."

Eva reached across the space between them and laid her hand on his shoulder. "You're a *goot* brother, and she is blessed to have you."

He covered her hand with his. "I'm glad you think so."

She pulled her hand away from his tender touch. "It's getting late. I should go in."

She stood up and so did he. They walked side by side toward her porch. She kept her fingers clasped tightly in front of her because she wanted him to take her hand more than anything. A simple stroll while holding hands wouldn't hurt anything, but it would change everything and she couldn't risk it. The last thing she wanted to do was to drive him away with her unwanted attention.

"Good night," she said then rushed inside without waiting for his reply.

The workers clattered into the schoolyard before dawn. Eva watched from her kitchen window as wagonloads of lumber were parked where there would be easy access to their cargo. Otto and Harley took the horses over to Willis's place. It was the closest corral.

Bishop Schultz was the one in charge as events unfolded. Eva kept a big pot of coffee hot and served anyone who asked for a cup. When a busload of Amish men arrived from a settlement in Pennsylvania to help she quickly put on another pot.

The bishop never appeared hurried or at a loss. To her it looked as if everybody knew exactly what to do. Danny and Harley were among those getting the walls in place. Willis was putting the new window in the school. Otto stood by with a caulk gun, ready to seal it when Willis got off the ladder. It made her smile to see the two of them working together.

By ten o'clock the framing for the four outer walls was going up. A long line of men hefted the first wall off the ground at a sign from Bishop Schultz. Some men used long poles to hoist it upright while an equal number of them quickly fastened it to the foundation. The ring of hammers filled the air.

A few minutes after ten the first buggy full of women arrived, followed by the bench wagon driven by Constance Schultz. The women quickly set out tables on the schoolhouse lawn and covered them with bright checkered cloths. Baskets of food were unloaded next.

Becca Beachy arrived with her daughter and her father-in-law. He walked with a pronounced limp and used a cane, but he soon had the young boys applying paint to the first finished wall. Annabeth and Maddie took their places on the swings until Dinah called them over to babysit the infants while their mothers began serving food.

Danny collided with Becca coming out of the house. She blushed and murmured an apology as she hurried away. Danny stood staring after her. Eva took note of the bemused expression on his face when he turned to her. "Who was that?"

"That is Becca Beachy. She and her father-in-law recently moved here."

"Oh, she's married, then."

"She's a widow. She has a little girl Maddie's age. Dinah said she is one of Samuel Yoder's grandchildren."

"Is that so? Well, I hope they like it here." He walked back out to the barn.

Eva glanced at him and then at Becca, who was watching him, too. Should she drop a hint that Danny wasn't a resident of New Covenant and that he would be leaving soon? She decided against it and went back inside to make more iced tea for those who wanted it instead of coffee.

Everyone was sitting down to eat when Dale Kaufman

pulled up in his yellow pickup. Jesse and Willis went down to the street to see what he needed. Willis came back to Eva a few minutes later. "Dale says he has a delivery for you. Four large crates. Where would you like them?"

Eva clasped her hands together in excitement. "They're here. My books are here. Take them inside the school, please." She wrapped her hands around Willis's arm and pulled him into the school. "I'm so excited to be able to share them with my students. I may even start a lending library so that the adults in this community can borrow them."

Dale brought in a crate and pried the top off. "Are these what you're waiting for?"

"Ja."

"I'll get the rest."

He went out and Eva grinned at Willis. "You may have the first pick and don't tell me you don't have time to read. You will this winter."

He slipped her hands off his arm. "Okay. I'll do that. Um, I know Harley likes to read. The kid always has his nose in a horse magazine. Maybe you could pick one out for him about horses."

"We'll each pick one for him." She drew her hand along the spines of the books. "Let's see I have *The Black Stallion, Black Beauty* and several Westerns featuring horses." She picked out one.

"Okay." Willis rubbed his hands on his pant legs.

She waited for him to look through her collection. What was wrong? He took a step back. It was almost as if he was afraid of them.

"I'm sure Harley will like whatever you choose. He can bring it back if he doesn't and pick another."

* * *

Willis swallowed hard and shook his head at Eva's excitement. All for a couple of crates of books. The joy on her face was unbelievable. There was no doubt about it. Eva didn't just like books. She loved them. Any man who wanted to woo her would do well to come visiting with a new book under his arm each time he stopped in.

And that man wouldn't be him. He could carry a crate of them, but he couldn't choose one. He wouldn't know if it was one Harley would like. If he picked the wrong book, would she guess he didn't know what he was looking at?

She was waiting for him to look them over. Watching him to see what he would do. He read the confusion in her eyes. She didn't know why he was hesitating. He rubbed a hand across his dry lips and leaned down.

He ran his fingers along them as he had seen her do. "I'll surprise him with this one." He pulled a book out and tucked it under his arm. "Now I've got to get back to work."

"Are you sure that's the one you want him to have?"

"Yup. See you later." He stumbled a little as he turned to go. His legs were stiff with fright.

Harley came through the door. "I heard the books came in."

"They did. I picked one out for you already. I hope you enjoy it." He pressed the book into Harley's hands, praying it was something that might interest him.

Harley took the book, looked around Willis to Eva and back to the book in his hands. He frowned slightly. "*Danki, bruder.* You must have heard me say I wanted to learn more about the history of Scotland."

Willis didn't realize he was holding his breath until

his brother finished speaking. He drew in a ragged gasp of air. "I did. Make sure you get it back to Eva when you are done with it."

He left the school thanking God that he had survived such a close call but his time was running out.

The exterior of the barn was finished by four o'clock. It was the traditional barn in shape but not in size, being only about one-third as big as the usual structures. When the interior was finished, it would hold ten horses or ponies in roomy stalls. The parents of the schoolchildren would be responsible for keeping hay and grain available. The older children in Eva's class would keep the stable clean and make sure there was water available for the animals during the day.

People were starting to leave when Willis went in search of Eva again. He found her sitting on the floor beside her bookcases with stacks of books surrounding her. "I came to tell you that I'm going home. Most of the workers have already left. What are you doing?"

She gestured to the stacks around her. "At first I put them out in alphabetical order but then I realized it would be better if I separated them into age-appropriate categories. Upon sorting, I realized that some of them are very hard to decide which age group would enjoy them the most."

She held up one of the books with a deep blue cover edged in gold. "Take *Anne of Green Gables*. Any age would enjoy this story."

"Decisions, decisions. All in a day's work for the schoolteacher. If you ask me, which you haven't, but I'm going to give you my opinion anyway, put the books that might fit any age on their own shelf. That way someone younger who reads it will feel quite an accomplishment and someone older who reads it won't feel like he or she is taking a book from the baby section."

"I don't have a baby section. Should I get one?"

"You should finish up and go take a look at your new barn."

"I believe it is actually the school's barn. Are you going to bring Dodger over tonight?"

"The corral isn't finished. He can stay with me a few more days."

"I appreciate all you have done for me, Willis."

He stood and hooked his thumbs under his suspenders. "Save your appreciation until after you get my bill." He held out his hand. She grasped it and he helped her to her feet.

It was a mistake on his part. Once her hand was nestled inside his, he didn't want to let go. The urge to draw her closer and kiss her sweet lips was overpowering.

How had he fallen so hard for this woman? He knew it couldn't work. Eva might not view him as a laughingstock the way the last woman he cared for had done, but she would be repulsed by his ignorance, and he couldn't stand seeing that in her eyes.

He made himself release her hand and he turned away from her. "The barn has plenty of room. You will be able to store your buggy inside when you get one. I'll keep an eye out for a used one if you don't have the funds for a new one."

"You must be joking. I don't have the funds for a new book let alone a new buggy. Does your *Ordnung* allow baptized members to ride a bicycle or a scooter?"

"Bicycles. But nobody rides them in the winter." They stepped outside of the school and the last of the building crew were out on the road walking home. A line of six men dressed in dark blue pants, matching jackets and straw hats.

"Hopefully, I will have a buggy before the first snow."

"That could be next week."

Her eyes grew wide. "Are you serious? You can have snow here in September?"

His gaze was drawn to her lips parted in surprise. And he wasn't going to think about kissing her. He wasn't. "It's happened. Late September, but we almost always have snow before Thanksgiving. Do you have snowshoes?"

"*Nee*, but I have big feet. Will that help?"

He checked out the small sneakers she was wearing. He wouldn't say she had big feet by any stretch of the imagination. "Buy snowshoes. I'll see you later." He started toward his house.

"Aren't you going to show me the barn?" she asked.

He turned around and pointed. "Behold. The barn. See you tomorrow."

He could make a joke out of it, but he wasn't laughing inside. He needed some distance between them. He needed to get his head straight and stop thinking about what it would be like to kiss the teacher.

Willis seemed in a big hurry to get away from her. Of course, she had no right to monopolize his time. It was simply that her world seemed empty when he wasn't in it. Instead of going into the house she chose to walk to the small grocery store at the other end of the community. New Covenant wasn't a true town. It was a string of Amish homes interspersed with a few *Englisch* ones along a narrow-paved road.

At the grocery store she purchased an array of fresh

vegetables and fruit. The prices were higher than what she was used to paying. Mr. Meriwether, the owner of the grocery, was a likable fellow who enjoyed visiting with his customers. As she was paying she noticed a small flyer on a bulletin board behind the cash register. It was for a cabinetmaker in Presque Isle, the largest city in Aroostook County. The phrase that caught her attention was "handmade cabinet pulls and knobs produced by local artisans."

"Mr. Meriwether, could I have that card?" She pointed out the one. "I'd like to write down their contact information."

He pulled the thumbtack out and handed the flyer to her. "The fellow's name is Ray Jackson. He comes here once or twice a month. I can easily get another one."

"Thank you. Is he local?"

Mr. Meriwether shook his head. "He's from Portland. He owns a couple of stores there, and one in Presque Isle. He comes out to get wood from your bishop. The one who makes backyard sheds and those ridiculous little houses. Bishop Schultz gets his wood from an Amish fellow who runs his own sawmill."

"Thank you again." She left the store and headed home. Perhaps Willis could sell his handmade cabinet knobs and pulls to this man. If he came to New Covenant monthly, Willis might not even have the expense of shipping his products to Presque Isle or Portland. She would suggest it. Perhaps the bishop could introduce the two. Feeling quite pleased with herself, Eva walked briskly all the way home.

Her brother was sitting at the kitchen table with a glass of milk and a sandwich. She grinned at him. "A man who knows how to make his own supper is a welcome addition to any household. I think I may have found a place for Willis to sell some of his ironwork."

Danny had an odd expression on his face. He didn't ask about her discovery. Instead, he held out an envelope. "You have a letter from Gene."

She put the brown paper bag with her groceries on the kitchen counter and took the letter from him. Was she being summoned home? She looked at Danny. "I don't want to read it. I don't want to go back to Illinois."

"I understand that but I'm not sure Gene will."

"Why? Why can't my life come first for a change?"

"I can tell you what he will say. Because we are commanded by our Lord to care for others. There isn't a commandment to make thyself happy first."

"There should be. Is there anything else?"

"A packet from a school in Maryland."

"*Goot.* Those must be the records for Otto and Harley." She laid her brother's letter on the counter. She picked it up and turned it over so she couldn't see her brother's handwriting. "I don't have to read it right away.

"I'm not going to be the one who tells you what to do. I can see how much you love—it here. I like it here."

She sat down at the kitchen table and clasped her hands together. "I appreciate that."

"So you found someplace for Willis to sell his iron-work?"

She turned away from the letter and smiled. "I saw this flyer in the grocery store. It is for a cabinet-making business. They have hand-wrought hardware. It would be helpful to the family if Willis could sell items on a regular basis and not just when a horse throws a shoe or a potato digger has a broken nose."

"Potato diggers have noses?"

"Sure." She put her hands together in front of her face. "It's the part that pushes into the ground underneath the potatoes and brings them up to the surface."

"Since when are you an expert on potato diggers?"

"I read about them when I knew I was going to come to this part of Maine. The potato is their main agricultural crop, but I don't want to talk about potatoes. I want to talk about finding a market for Willis's skills."

"I grant you the man knows how to work metal. I was thinking of taking some of his pieces back to Illinois to see if our company would be interested in using them. The downside of that will be the shipping cost. Finding a local market is a much better idea. And now you're going to open that letter from your brother so that I don't have to stay in suspense any longer."

"Very well, but if he wants me to come home, I'm not going to do it. I have a contract with the school board to be their teacher."

"I heard it was month-to-month, not a full year."

"So what? It's a contract." She stood up and picked up the letter. She slipped her finger under the envelope lip and ripped it open. She read the brief missive and burst into tears.

Chapter Thirteen

"Eva, please. You know I can't stand to see a woman cry." Danny was pushing a box of tissues into her hands. Eva dabbed her eyes with a handful and then blew her nose.

"Gene says I must come home at the end of this month. Corinne's mother is in a rehabilitation hospital. They expect her to return home by then." Eva struggled to control her sobs. "A month. That's all I have? It isn't fair."

"No one said life would be fair. I'm sorry. I really am. I think you would make a marvelous teacher."

"If I only have a month, then I will be a marvelous teacher for one month." She wiped her eyes and threw the tissue at the trash can. She missed. She bent over, picked up the tissue and dropped it in.

She pressed her lips together and looked at Danny. "*Nee*, I'm not going back. Gene will have to hire someone to take care of Corrine's mother. I will write him today and explain my reasoning."

"He's not going to like that. When have you ever known our brother to spend a penny more than he has to?"

Eva's bravado faded. "He can't force me to return."

"He can put a lot of pressure and guilt on you. Are you prepared for that?"

"I can't believe *Gott* would lead me all the way up here to simply send me home at the end of thirty days."

"I admire your spunk, but Gene won't. I'm sure he'll appeal to the bishop here."

She hadn't thought of that. If Bishop Schultz took Gene's side she would have no choice but to return home. Her job would vanish and her relationship with her family would be strained. Tears pricked her eyes again. Was her stubborn pride worth a rift with her family? She had aunts, uncles and cousins who would side with Gene because they believed that family came first.

Danny put his arm around her shoulder and gave her a hug. "A lot can change in a month. Maybe the good Lord will decide you belong here."

"Maybe. I'm going to write to Gene anyway." She wasn't going to lose hope.

"Will you tell Willis that you have been ordered home?"

Eva shook her head. "Not yet. He has been such a good friend to me. I will miss him more than I can say."

"He seems like a fine man."

She stepped to the sink and splashed water on her face. "I have a lot to do and not much time to do it in."

Would she be able to face Willis without breaking down? She had to. For his sake as well as for hers.

That evening she wrote a lengthy letter to Gene explaining why she needed to stay in Maine and continue teaching. She didn't mention Willis or how moving away from him and his wonderful family would break her heart.

After a troubled night's sleep, Eva was ready to face

the day, determined to enjoy what was left of her time in New Covenant if Gene's mind wasn't changed by her letter. The three children arrived in time for breakfast but Willis wasn't with them. Eva was grateful for the reprieve. She wasn't sure she could keep from crying. She made cinnamon rolls as a special treat for the children. A few minutes before eight o'clock, Harley left to go wherever Harley went. Eva, Otto, Danny and Maddie all went over to the schoolhouse.

She put Danny in charge of shelving the books and making note cards and note card holders so she could keep track of who had the books checked out. At least her books would be here if she was forced to leave. She prayed the children would find some solace in knowing she cared enough to leave her most prized possessions in their care.

"When is the first day of school?" Danny asked. He was on the floor thumbing through some of her books for the older students.

"It starts tomorrow at eight o'clock," she said, wondering if she was ready. "When will you be leaving?"

"The middle of the week."

She walked outside and returned a short time later with a shoebox lid. It held an inch of sand in the bottom. She sat down at her desk. "Otto, can you come here, please?"

He came over, looking at her with suspicion. "*Ja*, Teacher?"

"I know that you have had trouble reading and writing in school. Your records from you last school show it. I've consulted with some other teachers and we believe you may be suffering from dyslexia. It's a condition that makes it very hard to learn to read or write.

We can't say for sure that you have it but there are tests that can tell us for certain that you do. Would you be willing to be tested?"

"I don't know. Maybe. I should ask Willis."

"That's a good idea." She held up the little box. "In the meantime, I would like you to practice writing some letters in this sandbox instead of with paper and pencil. I want you to spell sand one letter at a time."

She scooted over to make room for him. "Come sit beside me. I'll help you."

"Is this the test?"

She smiled to reassure him. "*Nee*, this is a way to make learning easier for you."

"Why write them in the sand?" Danny asked.

"With dyslexia, a child's ability to identify a sound when they see the letter is impaired. This lets you see and feel the grains of sand as you work. It helps a different part of your brain remember the letter. Want to try it, Otto?"

Otto shrugged but he sat down with the box beside her desk. Eva smiled at him. "Let's start with the letter S." She drew it for him and she let him trace it over and over through the sand.

While Otto was doing that, she took Maddie to the bookshelf and allowed her to pick out a book for herself. She eagerly chose one and opened the book but there were words along with the pictures. She looked up at Eva. "I can't read this."

"I'll help you read it," Danny said.

"Are you as excited for school to start as I am? Can you believe it starts tomorrow?"

"I'm gonna walk to school. I don't think Willis is ever going to shoe my pony."

Eva felt she should defend him. "He's had many things to do. Some that you don't know about. He has to work hard to make enough money so you can eat and have a place to live."

Maddie mulled that over and nodded. "I guess my pony can wait. Will you remind him?"

"I will."

They had a lunch of peanut butter and jelly sandwiches along with fresh apples and some of the leftover cinnamon rolls. It was a little before four o'clock when Willis walked in the door.

Eva's heart expanded to fill her chest at the sight of his grimy face. Tears sprang to her eyes but she blinked them away. She didn't want to ruin any of their time together.

He looked around the room. "Where is Danny?"

She smiled. "He is out at the barn helping dig the post holes for the corral fence."

"Sounds like tough work. I should go help."

"Before you go I have something I want to show you." She handed him the flyer. He looked at it and turned it over once. "So?"

"This man sells hand-forged hardware and brackets for the kitchen cabinets that they make in their shop. He buys his lumber from Bishop Schultz. You should ask the bishop to give you an introduction. If this man likes your work, he can pick up the hardware when he comes to pick up the lumber. That way, neither one of you have to worry about the cost of shipping. What do you think?"

"I already have a lot to do, but I'll check with the bishop."

He didn't seem excited at the prospect. Eva dropped the subject. He scrutinized her face and she worried that some traces of her tears from last night might be remaining. "Are you okay?"

She managed a big smile this time. "Of course I am. I'm just stressed about starting school."

"You'll be fine. The kids will love you." He waved away her concern. Her fake grin faded. She longed to tell him she might be leaving but she kept silent. One of them hurting inside was enough.

Willis glanced at Otto as the two of them were cleaning up the kitchen after supper that evening. "The first day of school is tomorrow. Are you excited?"

"Not really." Otto slowly dried the plate in his hand.

Willis grunted. "I didn't care for school, either."

Otto looked at him. "Why?"

"It was hard for me. A lot harder than it was for my friends."

Otto went back to drying the plate. "That's the way it is for me, too. I'm just dumb, I guess."

"I've heard you described a lot of ways but I have never heard anyone call you *dumb*."

"Eva thinks I have something called dyslexia. Do you know anything about it?"

"I don't. What does Miss Eva say about it?"

"She wants me to have some tests to see if I've got it. I don't know. What good would it do?"

"Maybe they can cure it if they know what you've got." Was he giving the boy false hope?

Harley came into the kitchen. "I heard about it from one of the *Englisch* kids back home. He said his older brother had it. He was going to be tested because his grades weren't very good and sometimes it runs in families."

Willis turned to look at Harley. "You mean more than one person in the family can have it?"

"That's what he said."

"Did he get tested? Did he have it?" Otto asked.

"I never found out. We moved here, and I never saw him again."

Willis mulled over Harley's information. Was it possible he had this dyslexia thing along with Otto? It would explain a lot.

Maddie came out of her bedroom in her pajamas. She had a book under her arm. She held it up to Willis. "Eva gave me a book from her library. Will you read it to me, Willis?"

"I'm busy, not now." It was the same excuse he always used when he was confronted with something to read.

Her lips turned down in a frown. Willis wanted to read to her. He often made up stories for her. She didn't know they weren't the same words that were printed in the book he was looking at. But soon she would know and she would realize how ignorant her big brother was.

Harley reached over and took the book from her. "Come on, sprout. I'll read it to you." He looked at Willis and winked.

Willis's mouth fell open. He knew. Harley knew that Willis couldn't read. Shame left a bitter taste in his mouth. He had tried so hard to keep it a secret but a thirteen-year-old boy had figured it out. It made him wonder if Eva knew, too. He didn't think he could bear that.

"Do you think I should be tested?" Otto asked.

"I don't know."

"Harley, me and Maddie, we all like Eva a lot."

"I like her a lot, too." He sensed that there was something more to Otto's comment.

"Do you think you'll ever get married?"

"Why is everyone so concerned with my marital status? If I don't want to get married, I am not going to get married. That's the end of it." He hung his dish towel over the faucet and walked out of the room and out into the evening air.

The lights were off at Eva's home. He wanted to see her but he decided against it. He began walking out to the road and instead of following it, he crossed it and went up to the school. He laid a hand on the building. It had been built to last. Harley's grandchildren and great-grandchildren would stick their gum to the bottom of the seats, sing hymns and put on a Christmas play for their friends and family. He wished his experience had been different, but his childhood memories of school were mostly unhappy ones. He didn't want that for Otto or for Harley and certainly not for Maddie.

Willis turned his footsteps toward home but he didn't have enough willpower to pass by the schoolyard without checking to see if Eva was waiting on him on the swings.

She was.

He could still change his mind. He hesitated, but in the end he followed his heart and not his head. He sat down in the swing beside her. "You're up late."

"A little. I can't sleep."

"Nerves?"

She chuckled. "Exactly. That feeling of oh-what-have-I-gotten-myself-into? What has you walking the playground at this time of the night?"

"I have a lot of things on my mind." He got up and walked a few steps away. Then he turned to her again. "You are one of them."

"Me? Why do I trouble you?"

"Because I can't stop thinking about you."

"I think of you often, too."

He took a step closer. "I don't just think about you. I see you everywhere. I see you when I'm awake and I see you in my dreams. You're in all the things the kids tell me. I can see your eyes smiling at me from across the road."

She stared at the ground. "I'm sorry. I don't mean to be a distraction."

"That is exactly what you are." He walked toward her, bent down and kissed her. It was every bit as sweet as he had imagined it would be.

He moved his hand to the back of her head but she didn't draw away. She pressed her lips against his and slanted her face just enough to make their mouths fit together more perfectly. His heart started pounding so hard he knew she must hear it. Nothing had ever felt as right and as wonderful as her fingers when she laid her hands against his cheeks and let them slip into his hair. He thought he might die of happiness when she curled her fingers in his locks and held on.

Why couldn't he have been smarter, more deserving of her?

When he drew back he looked at her stunned face. She was so lovely, so kind and funny. Everything he ever dreamed of finding in a wife. Everything he knew he couldn't have.

He was struck with remorse. He couldn't give her false hope. "I'm sorry. I shouldn't have done that."

Eva pressed a hand to her mouth. "Don't say that. It was nice." She rushed away without another word.

Why did he have to do that? Eva hadn't been prepared. She stumbled toward her house. He wasn't supposed to kiss her. They were friends. Only it wasn't friendship that drew her to deepen the kiss and hold his face in her hands. She loved him. He had to know it now.

He wasn't supposed to say he was sorry afterward. How was she going to act from now on? He had changed everything.

It was her first kiss. He shouldn't have said he was sorry.

She could still feel the tingle on her lips. She stopped and looked back. He remained standing by the swings.

She rushed into her house being as quiet as possible. She didn't want Danny's sharp eyes noticing something was wrong. She didn't want to explain what had happened because she didn't understand it herself.

In her room, she sat down on the edge of her mattress and slowly took down her hair. What reason did Willis have for kissing her? She wasn't foolish enough to think her beauty had robbed him of coherent thought. Was she reading more into it? Had he simply followed an impulse because he felt sorry for her and then regretted it? Poor Eva, never been kissed?

That would be the most logical explanation. It didn't help her bruised ego. Tears filled her eyes. She was in love with Willis Gingrich and he was sorry he'd kissed her.

The sky was overcast but the rain held off for the first day of school. Some of the children arrived early enough to play outside on the playground equipment before coming in. The air was full of excitement, childish laughter and happy voices.

Eva greeted each of the students as they came in and introduced herself. Becca Beachy walked in with Annabeth. The little girl clutched her mother's hand. She did not want to go to school.

"I hope you don't mind if I sit in today," Becca said.

Eva shook her head. "Of course I don't mind. You may come as often as you wish."

Maddie came running up the steps, eager to choose her desk from the ones in the front row. "Morning, Teacher. Willis said Bubble had to stay at home or at least outside. He said a girl my age doesn't need an imaginary friend. I'm supposed to make real ones. Will you be my friend?"

Eva smiled and nodded. "I would love to be your friend. And I think Annabeth would also enjoy being your friend. Why don't you go sit by her? She's sort of scared today."

"There isn't anything to be scared of." Maddie tromped to the front of the room.

Eva was as prepared as she could be. She had written out exactly what needed to be done for every part of the morning and afternoon on a long list. That sheet of paper sat squarely in the middle of her desk so she could refer to it as needed. At exactly eight o'clock she rang the bell and everyone took their seats. The murmur of voices died away.

She wrote her name on the blackboard and turned around to face the class. She had never been more nervous in her life. Fifteen eager children watched her every move. Her mouth went dry. She wasn't going to be able to do this. What came next? She walked over to her desk only to discover her sheet of paper was gone. She checked underneath the desk and the chair but her list was nowhere to be found.

What next? She was going to blame Willis for making her so scatterbrained this morning. "Let's begin the day with a song."

One boy in the back held up his hand. "Shouldn't you begin with a prayer?"

"That's what I meant to say. A prayer. The Lord's Prayer."

Two of the girls from a newly arrived family rose to their feet. "*Daed* said we should all stand for a prayer."

"Of course. Everyone stand, please." As the class recited the prayer Eva prayed as hard as she could that she would make it through the day. What came next? Arithmetic assignments or reading with the first graders? When was recess?

"Amen," they all said in unison. Then they were all staring at her, waiting for directions and her mind was blank.

Eva sat on one of the swings in the schoolyard after the last of the children went home. She didn't want to return to Illinois, but she might not have a choice after this. Once Samuel Yoder heard about her first day of school, he was sure to start looking for a teacher who knew what she was doing.

"How did it go?"

She wasn't surprised when Willis came over and took a seat beside her. She had been hoping to see him. The need to confide her failure was overpowering as was the need to find out why he had kissed her.

"My first day on the job was a complete and utter disaster. I don't know why I ever thought I could be a teacher."

"Were the students unruly? Was Otto part of the problem?"

"I was the only problem. I had made a list of all the things I needed to do throughout the day and I lost that list five minutes after I rang the bell. I looked at all those faces waiting on me to do something and I panicked."

"That doesn't sound like the Eva I know."

"Before the first hour was up, two of the boys were involved in a paper wad fight, Annabeth was crying because she didn't want to be there and Sadie kept running into the room and barking at everyone."

"Keeping the door shut might have kept the dog out."

"Oh I tried that, but someone kept opening the door when my back was turned."

Tears stung her eyes. "I thought I could do this. I thought it would be easy. School was always easy for me. I never had to struggle over a problem the way Otto has to struggle. I don't know how to help him."

"You help him just by caring about him."

"I wanted all the children to love school the way I loved it."

"I hate to say this but maybe it's not about you."

She turned to gape at him. "I was the only one at the front of the schoolroom. How can it not be about me?"

"Shouldn't it be about your scholars? About what they need and not about what you used to do? Maybe your expectations were too high."

She pushed back and began swinging. "Well, they're not too high anymore. I'll be thrilled if any of the parents let their children come back for a second day."

"I think you're being too hard on yourself. Every big change takes some getting used to."

"I'm afraid I will give the children a disgust of education. I can imagine how the public school teachers will laugh at me when they hear about this. They go to four years of college or more to become teachers. I thought I could do it with a sharp pencil and a book of hymns."

He started swinging back and forth. "Maybe you're looking at teaching from the wrong angle."

"What's that supposed to mean?"

"What's the big picture?"

"I want Otto to be able to read. I want Maddie to learn her letters and numbers. I want the Yoder twins to stop shooting paper wads at each other and the other children."

"Those are all the little parts. You are looking at the cogs. You aren't looking at the driveshaft."

"Now you're talking over my head. What is the driveshaft?" She had been afraid she couldn't talk to him anymore but they were right back where they had been before the kiss. Or almost.

"A driveshaft is the big piece that turns all the small ones. Our Amish faith is the driveshaft. The Amish want to educate our children to be good stewards of the land and to care for each other. We want God first, family second and our community third. You need to look at your students in that light."

She stopped swinging. "How do I become a driveshaft?"

He chuckled. "First, you need a backbone of steel. The driveshaft has to be strong or it breaks and the whole machine becomes useless."

She wrapped her arms around the chains and rolled her eyes. "I can talk a good game but I'm not tough enough to say I have a backbone of steel."

"You're going to have to get one."

"Do you have a spare in your junk pile?"

He stopped swinging. "If I did I would give it to you

in a heartbeat. I'm afraid you're going to have to forge your own. It takes heat, time and patience before metal can be shaped. I'm going to guess it takes the same thing to shape scholars. You can't do it in one day. Just as I can't turn out a horseshoe with a single mighty blow of my hammer. It takes a lot of small strikes in just the right places to bend steel. You didn't have your iron hot enough today. It's a mistake all new blacksmiths make."

She drew a deep breath, buoyed by his words. "I'm going to find my list and stick to it tomorrow."

He got out of the swing and stood in front of her. He leaned down and tapped one finger against her forehead. "The knowledge you need is already in here. Your list is a useless crutch that can blow away in the wind. Your scholars need to believe you know more than they do." He stood up straight.

She nodded slowly. "I think you should be the teacher and I should go pound metal into crooked horseshoes."

He laughed. "If I find a horse with a crooked hoof I will call on you." He stopped laughing and grew somber. "Eva, about last night."

"I was wondering when that would come up."

"Can we forget it happened?"

"No."

He arched one eyebrow. "That wasn't the answer I had hoped for."

"You shocked me beyond belief."

"I shocked myself. I value you as a dear friend. You are an attractive woman and I got carried away. It won't happen again. You've heard me say I don't want to marry and that is true. I didn't mean to give you false hope or treat you poorly."

"Then I will say that I forgive you."

"*Danki*. Good night, Teacher."

"Good night." Eva was sorry to see him leave. She sat on the swing until the moon began to rise. Somehow, everything seemed better when she could talk it over with Willis. He had quickly become important in her life. That one kiss had opened her eyes to what she wanted and it was much more than friendship. She wanted his love in return. Foolish or not, she wanted to be held in his arms and kissed without an apology to follow. Was it possible? Or would she be gone before that happened?

Chapter Fourteen

The next school day Eva faced the classroom with new determination as she kept Willis's advice in mind. "Good morning, students."

"Good morning, Teacher," they said in unison.

"Let us stand and pray." She bowed her head.

When she finished she smiled at the classes. "Yesterday wasn't the best start to your new school year. Today will be better. Jenny Martin is going to be my helper. Jenny, I'd like you to assist the third and fourth grade students to do page one and two in their math workbooks. And make sure Sadie stays outside today."

"Yes, Teacher."

Eva looked to the two boys in the very last row. "If the dog comes in today we will all forgo recess. Do I make myself clear?"

The twins looked at each other and nodded. She smiled "*Goot.* Take your places for our singing."

Willis dropped by after school the next day to see how Eva was getting along. Maddie was playing with Sadie and Jenny in the schoolyard. He found both his brothers still inside at the blackboard. Eva looked up and smiled when she caught sight of him, and it warmed his heart. "How did things go today?" he asked.

"I took your advice and the day went better. It's going to take more than a few days for everyone to learn their schedules and to behave in a single classroom while I'm busy with other students."

She quickly changed the subject. "Have you contacted the cabinetmaker I told you about yet?"

"I spoke to him on the phone this morning. I have a meeting with him tomorrow. He has asked me to visit his businesses in Portland and bring samples of my work.

"That's wonderful."

It was and he was going to do his best to secure a new line of income to support his family. The thought of being away from Eva for two days was already depressing him. How was he going to go through life without kissing her again?

He cleared his throat. "Dale has agreed to drive me. We leave this afternoon. I'll be home late tomorrow night. I've arranged for the children to stay with Michael and Bethany while I'm gone and don't say you will keep them. You have enough to do."

He watched a wry smile curve her pretty lips. "I would happily take care them, but it would be a bit crowded with Danny here."

She was kind and generous, and he loved her. If he told her that he couldn't read would she react with compassion or recoil from his stupidity?

He needed to tell her. He didn't want any secrets between them.

He gazed at her sweet face and knew he would do it. He would find the courage. When he was back from

Portland with a contract for more work and a chance at a future together he would tell her when they were alone.

"I appreciate that you want to help," he said softly and pushed his hands into his pockets to keep from touching her face. She gazed intently into his eyes and then looked away as a faint blush rose to her cheeks. Was she remembering that evening? He wished he knew how she felt about him. When he found the courage to tell her about his problem, would she be as understanding and as kind to him as she was with Otto? How could he doubt that?

"I have work I must get done." Eva left his side to go back to her desk.

Harley was helping Otto write letters in colored chalk on the blackboard. The sound of someone calling outside caught his attention. Willis walked to the door.

"Who is it?" Eva asked from her desk.

"I don't know them. Two *Englisch* women."

Eva moved to stand beside Willis. "The shorter one is Mrs. Kenworthy. She teaches at the public school. I don't know the other woman."

Mrs. Kenworthy waved when she spotted them standing in the schoolhouse door. "It's good to see you again, Eva. This is a friend of mine, Janet Obermeyer. She's with the Early Learning Center. I was telling her about the child we believe has a learning disability and she wished to speak to you."

Janet was tall and slim with short, straight red hair. She wore a lavender pantsuit and carried a briefcase. Willis turned to Eva. "Is she talking about Otto? He doesn't have a learning disability. It doesn't help the kid to have folks tell him he's not as good as everyone else."

"You are right, sir," Janet said. "Labels are not useful. A proper diagnosis is."

"There's nothing wrong with my brother. He's as smart as anyone. Maybe smarter." He glanced at Otto. The boy looked ready to bolt.

"From what Mrs. Kenworthy has told me, I suspect your brother may be affected by dyslexia. Many people with dyslexia are of above-average intelligence. I have brought some educational materials with me."

She looked directly at Otto. "The problem isn't a lack of intelligence. The problem lies in the way the brain fails to interpret the connection between letters and words with the sounds that they should make."

"So I've got a bad brain. Is that it?" Otto scowled at her.

Willis heard the pain in his voice and wished he knew how to help. Had he been blind to Otto's struggle because of his own shame?

"Not at all," Janet said. "Some children excel at math, others don't. Some children are good at art, others are not. Those are only a few examples of how our brains function differently. None of which are bad."

"Exactly what is dyslexia?" Danny asked from behind Willis. He hadn't heard him come in.

"A good question but one without an easy answer," Janet said.

"This is my brother Danny," Eva said.

Janet handed several books to Eva and then turned to Danny. "Reading isn't natural. Speaking is. Reading requires our brain to match letters to sounds, put those sounds together in a correct order to create a word, and then form words together into the sentences we can read, understand and write again. People with dyslexia have trouble matching the letters they see with the sounds the letters and combinations of letters make."

"Can it be cured?" Eva asked.

Janet shook her head. "It can't be cured. It is a life-long problem, but with the right supports, dyslexic children can become highly successful students and adults."

Eva leaned forward eagerly. "How do I accomplish that?"

"The first step is by having a dyslexia-friendly classroom, one that encourages dyslexic students to find their strengths and follow their interests."

Eva sat back. "All this is new to me. Can you explain what you mean?"

"Dyslexic-friendly means things like using colors to highlight different parts of speech. One thing that has been found to be effective is tactile learning. By using something as simple as a tray of sand the student can say the letter and write the letter in the sand with his finger over and over. It reinforces learning in a different part of the brain."

"Teacher has been having me do that," Otto said.

The woman smiled. "Excellent start."

Willis listened intently to what the women were saying. What did it mean for him if he had this problem, too?

Mrs. Kenworthy looked straight at Otto. "Children with dyslexia often believe they are stupid, but they aren't. Not by a long shot."

Willis fought against the hope rising in his heart. Was it possible that he had dyslexia and that was why he couldn't read? Maybe he wasn't ignorant or stupid. Maybe it was because his brain didn't recognize the squiggly lines as words. After all the years of believing he was inferior it was hard to wrap his mind around the fact that he might not be.

If he could learn to read, he could hold his head up in front of a congregation and preach from the Good Book. He could take a wife and not worry that she would be ashamed of him. It would mean he could keep better records for his business. It meant he could admit his love for Eva. The hope unfolding in his chest was almost painful.

"What else should I do?" Eva asked.

"Read aloud to your students. Show them your love of reading and books. Make it part of every school day. Encourage the parents to do the same."

Danny leaned against the corner of Eva's desk. "Are there some things that a teacher shouldn't do?"

"Never ask a dyslexic child to read aloud in front of classmates. It only serves to shame and embarrass them. We are learning more about this problem every year. Thousands of people live with this disorder. Most of them go on to become successful individuals. But it takes a lot of work."

"What about a grown-up who has dyslexia?" Harley asked. "Can they learn to read?"

Janet nodded. "Many young adults with dyslexia do learn to read but not rapidly or easily."

Harley frowned. "But if they can't read at all, can they learn with help?"

Janet smiled sadly. "It is much more difficult to retrain an adult brain. It can be done but it takes years of work and therapy. Even with that it is unlikely that they will be proficient readers."

Willis swallowed hard. The memory of the humiliation he had endured in school and from his so-called friends burned in the pit of his stomach.

"But it is possible?" Harley asked looking at Willis.

Janet nodded. "It is possible."

Willis rubbed his hands on his pant legs. He wasn't afraid of hard work. Not if a life with Eva was his reward.

Eva caught Willis smiling at her and she had to look away from the warmth in his gaze for fear she would start blushing. She was afraid the others would notice so she hugged the books Janet had given her to her chest.

Willis cleared his throat. "I'd better get going."

Eva followed him to the door. "When you get back from Portland will you put shoes on Maddie's pony? She is constantly asking me to remind you."

Willis's smile disappeared. He looked at her with sorrow-filled eyes. "Maddie doesn't have a pony anymore. Her pony was pulling the cart when her *Mamm* and *Daed* were struck by a semi. Her pony was killed, too."

Eva pressed a hand to her heart. "The poor baby. No wonder she has a make-believe friend. Bubble can't be hurt."

"Thanks to you she is making real friends again. When I get back I have something I need to tell you."

She tipped her head to the side. "Can't you tell me now?"

"*Nee*, when we are alone," he said quietly with a glance at the others watching them. He settled his hat on his head and left.

That evening Eva went to the swing set instead of staying at home. She knew Willis was gone. She had seen him leave with Dale in his yellow pickup an hour ago. She prayed Willis's trip would be successful. He was determined to provide for his family, and she loved him for it.

She pushed herself back and forth with one foot as darkness descended. The swing was the place she felt closest to Willis. She missed his engaging conversations more than anything. She missed the way he looked her and the way he smiled at her. She touched her lips with her fingertips. Would he ever kiss her again? He cared. She knew that, but was it love? Was that what he wanted to tell her? She hugged her secret hope close to her heart.

When she entered the house sometime later she found Danny raiding her cookie jar with a tall glass of milk in one hand. His eyebrows drew together. "Where have you been?"

"Enjoying the evening. Why are you still up?"

"I just wanted to tell you I understand why you are drawn to teaching, Eva. I never thought about it before, but I see how rewarding it can be. You have opened my eyes."

"*Danki*. Hand me a cookie, please."

He held one out. "Eat it first, and then I'll tell you about your letter."

"From Gene?"

"Yup."

"Put my cookie back. I've lost my appetite. Where is it?"

"On the table by your rocker."

"Did you open it to see what he says?"

"I don't open other people's mail. What kind of snoop do you think I am?"

"I'm sorry. When will you be leaving?"

"The day after tomorrow."

"I'll miss you."

"Look on the bright side. You might be coming with me."

His joke wasn't funny. She went into her sitting room

and picked up the letter. Drawing a deep breath, she slit it open and read her brother's brief note. He was expecting her to come home with Danny as soon as possible. He had included the money for a bus ticket this time.

"And?" Danny asked.

"I made myself plain in the letter I sent him. I want to stay. He's enclosed the money for our bus tickets and says he has written to the bishop and the school board detailing why I shouldn't be a teacher and why I'm needed at home. I lose. Gene wins."

"Gene's going to be eating burnt pancakes for the rest of his life, isn't he?"

"Very likely."

"I'm sorry, sis."

"I know."

He walked away. Eva stared at her letter. Danny might calmly accept Gene's order to return home, but she wasn't going to leave unless she had no other choice.

The next day started off well at school. She confiscated the rubber bands from the Yoder twins and made Sadie go home the first time she poked her nose in the door. Both Harley and Otto were quiet but that was a good thing. The children went out for the morning recess and Eva stayed in to grade papers.

She didn't see what started the fight. One moment the children were playing a game of softball and when she looked up again there was a fistfight in progress. Otto and Harley were pummeling the Yoder twins.

She rushed out the door to break up the fight. She stepped between the two boys to push them apart. The next second she found herself in the dirt between them. Otto tripped over her legs and fell on top of her.

Before she could get up, the boys were pulled apart

by Bishop Schultz and Samuel Yoder. "What's going on here?" Yoder demanded.

"I haven't the least idea," Eva said breathlessly as she scrambled to her feet. The bishop had a hold of both Harley and the older Yoder boy.

"Grandson, what is the meaning of this?" Samuel demanded.

"Nothing." The boy couldn't look his grandfather in the eye.

Harley's face was beet red. "He called my brother an idiot, and he wouldn't take it back."

Samuel glared at Eva. "Is this the sort of behavior you are teaching our children?"

Her temper flared. "It is not. Your grandsons had learned to throw insults and punches long before I came."

"Woman, where is your *demoot*?"

She forced herself to calm down. "I beg your pardon. My humility is in short supply at the moment."

The bishop turned to the children gathered in a semi-circle. "School is dismissed early today. Go home."

They all filed away except for Harley, Otto and Maddie who gathered close to Eva. Jenny and little Annabeth waited by the school steps.

Eva managed a smile for the Gingrich children. "Go to the house, get cleaned up, do your chores then go home with Jenny. Bethany and Michael are expecting you to stay with them another night aren't they?"

Harley nodded. "Willis said he wouldn't be home until after midnight and he didn't want to get us so late on a school night."

"Okay, I will see you all tomorrow and we'll discuss what happened with him. Harley, my brother Danny is working in the new barn. Tell him Annabeth needs a ride home. She's too small to walk so far alone."

Samuel scowled at her when the children were gone. "It is as your brother Gene stated in his letter to us. You are not a proper teacher if you allow the *kinder* to engage in fistfights. You were warned that your contract would run for one month at a time, but an exception must be made. Consider yourself terminated."

"What?" Her jaw dropped.

"Samuel, I think you are being hasty," the bishop said calmly.

"I don't believe I am. Your pay will be forwarded to your home in Illinois. I will take over your duties until a suitable replacement can be found."

The two men walked off, leaving Eva reeling. She had lost her job and her home in one fell swoop. Her days in Maine had come to an end. All that she had feared was coming true.

She went back inside the school and stared at the blackboard. What was she to do? She needed to talk to Willis, but he wouldn't be back until late. She didn't want to wait until tomorrow to speak to him.

She grabbed a pen and a sheet of paper. The time for maidenly reserve was past. She was in love with Willis. If he cared for her, she would defy Gene and find a way to stay in Maine but she had to know for sure.

My dearest Willis,
I have been fired from my position as teacher. I don't want to leave you and the children. I love you Willis. I love Harley, Otto, Maggie and even Bubble. If you hold any feelings for me in your heart please meet me tonight at the swing set no matter

what time it is. I'll be waiting. I can't leave without knowing how you truly feel. Your kiss gave me hope even if that wasn't your intention.

If you don't come, I will know my hope was in vain and I will leave.

Eva

She sealed the letter and went to Willis's house. The children had already gone. She placed the note on the counter under the kerosene lamp where he couldn't miss it and left.

She told Danny what had happened when he returned from taking Annabeth home. He was as astonished as she had been. "What are you going to do?" he asked.

"I'll let you know in the morning." It all depended on Willis.

Time dragged until it was almost midnight. She hurried to the schoolyard and waited.

It was long before she heard Dale's truck pull in. She saw Willis enter his house. The light came on in the kitchen. Her heart began hammering in her chest. He had to be reading her letter. What was he thinking? Had she been too bold? The chains of swing bit into her palms as she waited. He must love her. She loved him so much.

He came out a short time later and went into his smithy without looking her way. She waited, afraid to breathe. When he came out of his workshop he went back into the house. Was he ignoring her request? His light went out.

She waited for another half hour and then bowed her head as the bitter truth sank in. He wasn't coming. He didn't love her. The tears she'd been holding back slipped free.

She made her way home, drying her eyes when she saw Danny was waiting up for her. "Well?"

"I'm going back with you."

"Tomorrow?"

"The sooner the better." She had been such a fool.

Chapter Fifteen

Willis couldn't wait to share his good news with Eva, but he didn't want to interrupt her during school. He'd been hired to supply all the hand-forged hardware for Ray Jackson's shops in Portland and for his new store in Boston. Willis decided to wait until he knew Eva would be free at lunch. In the meantime he got busy on Mr. Jackson's first order.

It was almost noon when he crossed the road and headed for the schoolhouse. He noticed a van stop in front of Eva's house. Bethany and Michael's buggy pulled up behind it. Dinah and Gemma got out along with Bethany and Michael. They went up to Eva's house. Was Danny heading back today? Willis would make sure to tell him goodbye, but he had to see Eva first.

He opened the door of the schoolhouse and stepped inside. Samuel Yoder sat at the desk up front. Otto was standing beside him with his hands clenched into fists at his sides. He was shaking and there were tears on his cheeks.

Willis strode to the front of the room. "What's going on? Otto, what's wrong?"

"Your brother is being stubborn. He has refused to read his assignment out loud."

Otto looked at Willis. "I can't."

Willis nodded. "I understand. It's going to be okay." He looked at Samuel. "Where is Eva?"

"Eva Coblentz no longer teaches here."

Willis wasn't sure that he heard right. "What do you mean she doesn't teach here? Where is she?"

"Preparing to return to Illinois with her brother."

"She wouldn't leave without telling me."

But maybe she had told him. He thought of the note he'd found on the counter last night. He had brought it with him to have Harley read it when they were alone.

Willis pulled the envelope from the pocket of his jacket and stared at it. She wouldn't have written a good-bye letter. She would've come to see him in person. Wouldn't she? He had to know if the note was from her. He held it out to Harley. "Read it."

Samuel scowled at them. "Willis, I am trying to conduct class here. If you have business with your brother, please step outside. Otto, read the statement on the board. You will not return to your seat until you have done as I asked, even if you have to stand here all day."

Harley came to Willis's side, pulled the letter out of the envelope and opened it. "My dearest Willis." Harley's eyes grew round. "I don't think I should read this. It's kind of personal."

"Is it from Eva?"

"*Ja.*"

Willis took the page from his brother. "*Danki.* Otto, Maddie, we're leaving."

Samuel rose to his feet. "Willis, you are interfering

with the discipline of this classroom. Your brother is not dismissed."

"If you were half the teacher that Eva Coblentz is, you would know that Otto suffers from dyslexia. Did you even bother to read her notes about the boy? He can't read his assignment. With special tutoring he will be able to someday, but humiliating him will not hasten that day. Come on, kids, we have to stop Eva."

Maddie was already headed for the door. Willis, followed closely by Otto and Harley, hurried to catch up with her. Outside he saw Danny loading a pair of suitcases into the van. Eva stood beside him. She was hugging Bethany. Michael shook hands with Danny while Dinah and Gemma looked on.

Fear choked Willis and closed his throat so he could barely breathe. What if she didn't want to stay? Why would she consider marrying a man as dimwitted as he was? She could have the choice of any man. A man who could read the books she loved and talk to her about them. He didn't deserve her.

Maddie tugged on his hand. "Come on. What are you waiting for?"

"I guess I'm waiting for my courage to show up."

"I don't think you're gonna find it standing here. You have to make Eva stay."

He smiled at his little sister. "I think I would rather face a bear than tell her what's wrong with me, but she has to know."

Eva had her black traveling bonnet on. She hadn't seen him. Willis crossed the strip of grass and ran up to the van where Danny was loading her belongings. "Eva, wait. What are you doing?"

When she looked his way, he saw her eyes were red

from crying. He wanted to take her in his arms and comfort her but he didn't know if she would allow it.

Tears glistened on her lashes. "I'm going home."

"But why? I thought you liked it here. I thought you loved teaching the children." He took hold of the van door.

I thought maybe you loved me.

She closed her eyes. "I explained why in my letter. I said everything there was to say. I don't want to rehash it here. Please, just let me go. You've been a fine friend and I'm sorry I expected more than you could give. Goodbye, Willis Gingrich. God be with you, always."

She was going to leave him unless he could put his pride and fear aside and make her understand. Her friends stood a few feet away watching him. Willis swallowed hard. Everyone would know what a failure he was, but he was more afraid of losing Eva. "I couldn't read your letter."

"I'm sorry if it embarrassed you. The feelings are my own and I understand that you couldn't return them."

He held the paper out to her. "You didn't hear me, Eva. I wasn't embarrassed by your letter because I couldn't read it. I can't read." He closed his eyes and hung his head.

Please, dear God, don't let her laugh.

The silence stretched on so long that he finally looked up. There were tears running down her cheeks. "Oh, Willis, why didn't you tell me?"

"I was ashamed. I didn't want anyone to know. I've hidden it for so long I didn't know how to tell you. I didn't want you to feel sorry for me. I didn't want you to know how stupid I was."

"I'm sorry you didn't feel you could trust me."

Willis gazed into her beautiful green eyes. "I wanted to."

This was the hard part. He stared at his feet. "When I was twenty, I started seeing a girl who wasn't Amish. She ran around with a cool bunch of kids. They had fast cars and money to spend, they liked loud music, but I think they were bored a lot of the time."

He stared at his hand on the car door. His knuckles were white from gripping the steel. Even now it hurt to repeat what happened. "I confided to that young woman that I couldn't read. I didn't want to keep a secret that big from someone I thought I was serious about." He swallowed hard.

"Go on," Eva said gently.

"She laughed a little. She thought I was kidding. She told the others. They laughed a lot. Of course I laughed, too. I pretended it didn't matter. A few days later we were coming back from a party when the boy driving pulled into a convenience store parking lot. He said he needed a few things, some candy, some crackers and soda. He gave me a twenty-dollar bill and a list of what he wanted. He said give it to the clerk and he'd get the stuff for me. So I went in and handed the young woman behind the counter the note." Willis stopped talking. Humiliation burned deep in his chest.

He felt a hand on his arm. Eva was staring at him intently. "It wasn't a list of grocery items, was it?"

"It read, *This is a holdup. Give me all the money in the cash drawer.*

"The clerk was just a kid. She went pale as a sheet, started shaking and crying. An alarm went off. I didn't know what was going on. Then my friends rushed in, laughing like a bunch of fools." He could see their red faces, hear them howling with mirth while they clapped him on the back as if he was somehow privy to the gag.

"They bolted when the police came." His girlfriend had been the first one out the door.

"I spent the next twelve hours explaining to them that I had been duped. I was fortunate that I didn't get arrested. I knew the story would be all over the county in a few days. I decided to leave before I had to face everyone. I ended up here. I never told anyone else, although recently there was someone that I wanted to confide in. The trouble is that she's so smart I was afraid she would be ashamed of me."

Eva stepped forward and cupped his face with her hands. "Willis, you are one of the finest men I have ever known. I love you. Do you hear me? I could never be ashamed of the man I love.

"You are not ignorant. When I think of all the times I criticized you for not caring about Otto's education I'm the one who is ashamed. I'm so sorry. Please forgive me."

He drew her into his arms without caring who saw. "There's nothing to forgive unless you leave this brokenhearted fellow behind and return to Illinois."

"Danny, take my things out of the car, please." Her eyes never left Willis's face. He started to believe she truly did love him.

Danny set her suitcases aside. "Why don't I take the kids to the bus station with me? The driver can bring them back here after we've said our goodbyes and had some ice cream. Who wants an ice cream cone?"

Maddie held up her hand. "I do. I do."

Harley put a hand on her head and turned her toward the van. "We all want some. Come on, Otto."

"Did you hear what Willis said? I'm not the only one. He's like me."

Harley ruffled Otto's hair and winked at Willis. "Yeah, I heard. I think our big brother's a mighty fine fellow. I hope he knows how blessed he is to have found a good teacher." The children got in the van with Danny and drove away.

Willis suddenly realized he was holding Eva in his arms in plain sight of the school, and a number of their church members. He looked over Eva's head at Michael. "I'd like to continue this conversation somewhere more private."

"We're going. Eva, you are welcome to stay with us for as long as need be," Michael said.

Dinah was grinning from ear to ear. "Leroy and I will make the same offer."

"*Danki.* You are all very kind."

They left and Eva turned to Willis. "Come into the house. I can make us some coffee although it actually belongs to the school and not to me. How did your meeting with the Bartlett people go?"

"I almost forgot. I have a standing order for two hundred cabinet pulls and hinges for the next two months. If they sell well, there will be more orders. They like them."

"I don't see why not. You do beautiful work."

As soon as they were in the house, he closed the door and pulled her into his arms again. "I'm going to kiss you, Eva Coblentz, unless you tell me I can't."

"I thought you'd never ask, Willis." She slipped her arms around his neck and closed her eyes.

Eva had dreamed about this moment since the first time they sat on the swings together. She knew then that she was losing her heart to this amazing man, though she had been too afraid to admit it. Their first kiss had been amazing. This kiss was far more wondrous.

His lips were firm and gentle as they touched hers. A shiver raced down her spine and she leaned closer, melting against him, loving the way he made her feel cherished and as giddy as any teenager. He pulled away with a sigh and tucked her head under his chin. "Have I told you how much I love you?"

"I'm not sure. I don't think you mentioned it."

"Eva darling, I love you. Today, tomorrow, for the rest of my life and into eternity, I will always love you."

She would never tire of hearing those words or of saying them. "I love you, too. What did I do to deserve such happiness?"

"I am asking myself the same question. I reckon only God knows for sure. Or maybe Bubble does."

"*Gott* has truly blessed us." She rose on her tiptoes to press a kiss to his lips. "What does Bubble have to do with any of this?"

Wrapping his arms around her, he pulled her closer and kissed her until her head was spinning and she was breathless all over again. Pulling away, he took a deep breath. "Bubble gave me some interesting encouragement."

Eva settled her face against the side of his neck. He smelled of smoke and leather and the pine forests all around them. She breathed in the scent knowing she would never forget it. "What sort of encouragement did an imaginary girl give you?"

"You'll laugh."

"At you? Never. With you? Every chance I get."

"Bubble told me you would say yes if I proposed to you."

"She did? Isn't she a bold child?"

He leaned back so he could see her face. "Maybe, but sometimes she spouts the truth when I'm least expecting it. Was she right?"

"I don't know."

"What do you mean you don't know?"

She looked up and tapped his nose with her finger. "You have not asked me."

He held her at arm's length. "Teacher, will you do me the honor of becoming my wife?"

"To have and to hold?"

He cupped her face with his hands. "In sickness and in health, *ja*, all of that. Will you please marry me? I desperately need someone to help me with the children and I need a good cook."

She pulled his hands away. "I knew you had an ulterior motive."

"I'm simply going down the list the *kinder* made. You're pretty and you aren't too old."

She laughed out loud. "I love you, Willis Gingrich and all your family."

A knock at the door startled them both. Willis moved a few steps away. Eva straightened her *kapp* and smoothed the front of her dress. She opened the door. Samuel Yoder stood there with a manila folder and his hand.

He cleared his throat. "I believe there has been a mistake. And I'm afraid that I am the one who has made it."

"Won't you come in?" Eva said. What was this about?

Samuel stepped to the door and nodded to Willis. "I finished reading your file on young Otto."

"I see. Please have a seat." She led the way to her sitting room and sat down in her rocking chair. Samuel sat on the edge of the sofa while Willis stood in the doorway, leaning one shoulder against the doorjamb.

Samuel looked from one to the other. "I was unaware of Otto's difficulties and I humiliated him in front of the other children. I want to apologize. In looking through your desk I saw numerous articles about dyslexia. Clearly, you have a plan to help the boy. I don't want to rob him of his chance to learn. I hope that you will consider returning to your teaching post. I will write to your brother and explain that you can't be spared at this time. If you want to stay?"

Eva's heart gave a little leap of joy. She glanced at Willis before replying.

"Your decision," he said with that adorable little half smile on his lips.

She folded her hands together tightly. "I will consider it."

The outside door opened. The children followed by Danny tripped into the kitchen with ice cream cones in their hands. They made themselves at home around the table. Danny looked into the sitting room. "Are we interrupting?"

Eva stared at him in amazement. "Did you miss your bus?"

"Nope. I saw it. I bought my ticket. I put my suitcase on it and then I changed my mind. Fortunately, I was able to get my suitcase off before the bus left. And I got a refund for the ticket."

"You're staying here? In New Covenant? Why?"

"I had a sneaking suspicion that there was going to be an opening for a new teacher soon. Also, Bubble mentioned that you were getting married. Can I guess who the poor fellow is?"

"Willis," Maddie called out. "Bubble said so."

Willis wagged his eyebrows at Eva. "Bubble is right again."

Danny handed his melting cone to Eva. "Brother Yoder, I'd like to talk to you about a teaching position. Have you considered hiring a man?"

"Having a man as a teacher is most unusual." Samuel stroked his beard. "But I will bring this to the attention of the school board."

"Fine. And is your granddaughter Becca seeing anyone?"

Samuel frowned. "My granddaughter?"

"I was just curious. Come, I'll walk you out." The two men went out the door, leaving Eva and Willis with the three children.

Willis tipped his head toward the kitchen. "I have some explaining to do. Care to listen?"

She walked up to him and laid her hand on his cheek. "If you are sure you don't mind?"

"I never want to keep secrets from you again."

Willis took a deep breath and sat down at the table with his brothers and his sister. "You heard me tell Eva that I can't read."

"Is it true?" Maddie asked.

"It is."

"But you read me stories at night sometimes."

"I only look at the pictures in your book and I make up the story as I go along. I'm not reading."

"You could have fooled me," she declared and licked her ice cream.

He saw Eva struggling not to laugh. "I fooled a lot of people. In school I could memorize what the other children read and then repeat it when my turn came. If I had to go first, I couldn't do it. Like Otto, I misbehaved a lot, hoping the teacher wouldn't notice. It worked for a while. She thought I was lazy and so did our *daed*."

"I guess he yelled at you a lot. He did me," Otto said quietly.

"He didn't understand what was wrong with us but he wanted the best for you and for me. I believe that. I wish he was still here so Eva could explain."

"He understands now," she said softly.

Willis nodded. "I started skipping school before the end of my last year and went to work in the smithy with my uncle. I didn't need to read there, and I liked it."

Harley walked to the front door. "I've got to go. Maddie, wait here. I'll be back in a minute." He took off at a run.

"What is that boy up to?" Willis asked.

The other two children shrugged. They all walked out onto the porch. Willis slipped his arm around Eva's waist and pulled her close. She pushed his arm away. "Not in front of the children," she whispered but she was smiling.

Harley came walking up the drive, leading a black-and-white pony. He stopped at the foot of the steps and waved to Mrs. Arnett. She waved back and pulled away in her truck with a horse trailer hooked on behind.

Harley handed the reins of the pony to Maddie. "I know you miss Popcorn. This is Zip. He's as sweet as they come and he's for you."

"For me?" Maddie squeaked.

"I've been working over at her farm so I could buy

him from Mrs. Arnett. Willis put shoes on him not long ago so you can ride him now if you'd like."

Maddie threw her arms around him. "You are the best brother ever!"

"I know. It was Otto's idea. He can't read well but he's the thinker in this family."

Maddie hugged Otto. "You are the second-best brother in the whole world."

"Sure, sure. Get up on him and go for a ride."

Willis lifted her to the pony's back and settled her feet in the stirrups. She beamed at him and Eva. "I'm going to go show Annabeth."

Eva pointed up the road. "Fourth farm on the left. There is a path along the edge of the woods so you don't have to ride out on the highway."

Willis nodded. "*Goot*. Okay. You and Bubble have a nice ride."

"She can't come. She's gone to visit her sister in Texas." Maddie turned Zip around and trotted him along the path that led past the school.

Harley tugged on Otto's arm. "Come on. We should keep an eye on her in case she decides to ride to Texas and show Bubble her new horse."

"Where is Texas?" Otto asked as he followed his brother.

Willis didn't hear Harley's reply. He turned to Eva and took her hand. Together they walked to the swing set beside the school. She sat down and he gave her a gentle push. He kept her swinging for a few minutes. "Do you want to continue teaching this year?"

She titled her head back to see him. "How did you know?"

"Bubble told me."

"How could she? She's in Texas."

"She mailed me a letter. Speaking of letters, do you want to read the one you wrote to me?"

"No."

"Why not?"

"Because I said some very personal things. I want you to read it for yourself someday."

"What if I can't ever do that?"

She put her feet down, hopped off and twisted around to look at him. "You will. It may take a long time and it won't be easy but I know you will."

"How can you be so sure?"

"Because you have a teacher who loves you. Do you mind if I finish out the school year here?"

"Maybe just a little but I know you had your heart set on it. I've waited for you my whole life. I can wait until school is out in the spring. But not one week more."

"I love you for that!" She leaned forward and he had no choice but to kiss her again.

It was much too brief. He foresaw a long winter ahead. "Was your brother serious about becoming a teacher?"

"I think he is. I'll have him be my helper this year and he can take over next year."

Willis moved the swing out of the way. "It's hard to believe this is real." He reached out and drew his fingers along the curve of her cheek. "I'm afraid I will wake and find it has all been a dream. Promise you won't vanish with the dawn."

She captured his hand and pressed a kiss into his palm. "I am not a dream. I love you, Willis, with all my heart. For now and forever. I thought this kind of love was found only in books but I was wrong. It's found in the heart. My heart."

She slipped her arms around his waist and laid her cheek against his chest.

He sighed deeply as he pulled her close. "I don't know anything about books or poems. All I know is iron and roaring hot coals. What will we talk about?"

She giggled and rose on tiptoe until her lips were only an inch away from his. "Silly man. Who says we're going to be talking? I plan on a lot of kissing and being kissed. Like this." She proceeded to show him just how wonderful a conversation with the teacher could be.

* * * * *

If you enjoyed this visit to the
North Country Amish, look for
the other books in the series:

An Amish Wife for Christmas
Shelter from the Storm

Dear Reader,

I hope you enjoyed the story of Eva and Willis. This is the second time in my career I have created a character who can't read. The first time was in my very first Love Inspired novel back in 2006 called *His Bundle of Love*. In that book it was the heroine. In this book I chose the hero because I wanted to show that sometimes strong men may not know how to ask for help. Willis was a blacksmith, a man of faith and willing to take on raising his siblings, but he was ashamed of what he thought was his defect.

I think some of us are like Willis. We love our faith and our family and we work to keep everything together. People may even see us as the "strong one," but inside we can be hurting. Maybe it's depression. Maybe it's worry over money or a failing marriage or an illness. At times we hide things from our family in order to protect them. So many times we think we can tough it out. Just get through it.

False pride kept Willis silent and he almost lost the love of his life. Don't let false pride keep you from finding peace of mind. Ask for help if you need it. I promise no matter what is wrong, you aren't alone.

Many blessings,

Patricia Davids

AN AMISH EASTER WISH
Green Mountain Blessings • by Jo Ann Brown
Overseeing kitchen volunteers while the community rebuilds after a flood, Abby Kauffman doesn't expect to get in between *Englischer* David Riehl and the orphaned teenager he's raising. Now she's determined to bring them closer together...but could Abby be the missing ingredient to this makeshift family?

THE AMISH NURSE'S SUITOR
Amish of Serenity Ridge • by Carrie Lighte
Rachel Blank's dream of becoming a nurse took her into the *Englisch* world, but now her sick brother needs her help. She'll handle the administrative side of his business, but only temporarily—especially since she doesn't get along with his partner, Arden Esh. But will falling in love change her plans?

THE COWBOY'S SECRET
Wyoming Sweethearts • by Jill Kemerer
When Dylan Kingsley arrives in town to meet his niece, the baby's guardian, Gabby Stover, doesn't quite trust the man she assumes is a drifter. He can spend time with little Phoebe only if he follows Gabby's rules—starting with getting a job. But she never imagines he's secretly a millionaire...

HOPING FOR A FATHER
The Calhoun Cowboys • by Lois Richer
Returning home to help run the family ranch when his parents are injured, Drew Calhoun knows he'll have to work with his ex—but doesn't know that he's a father. Mandy Brown kept his daughter a secret, but now that the truth's out, is he ready to be a dad?

LEARNING TO TRUST
Golden Grove • by Ruth Logan Herne
While widower Tug Moyer isn't looking for a new wife, his eight-year-old daughter is convinced he needs one—and that her social media plea will bring his perfect match. The response is high, but nobody seems quite right...except her teacher, Christa Alero, who insists she isn't interested.

HILL COUNTRY REDEMPTION
Hill Country Cowboys • by Shannon Taylor Vannatter
Larae Collins is determined to build her childhood ranch into a rodeo, but she needs animals—and her ex-boyfriend who lives next door is the local provider. Larae's not sure Rance Shepherd plans to stick around...so telling him he has a daughter is out of the question. But can she really keep that secret?

SPECIAL EXCERPT FROM

LOVE INSPIRED
INSPIRATIONAL ROMANCE

Temporarily in her Amish community to help with her sick brother's business, nurse Rachel Blank can't wait to get back to the Englisch *world...and far away from Arden Esh. Her brother's headstrong carpentry partner challenges her at every turn. But when a family crisis redefines their relationship, will Rachel realize the life she really wants is right here...with Arden?*

Read on for a sneak preview of
The Amish Nurse's Suitor *by Carrie Lighte,*
available April 2020 from Love Inspired.

The soup scalded Arden's tongue and gave him something to distract himself from the topsy-turvy way he was feeling. As he chugged down half a glass of milk, Rachel remarked how tired Ivan still seemed.

"*Jah*, he practically dozed off midsentence in his room."

"I'll have to wake him soon for his medication. And to check for a fever. They said to watch for that. A relapse of pneumonia can be even worse than the initial bout."

"You're going to need endurance, too."

"What?"

"You prayed I'd have endurance. You're going to need it, too," Arden explained. "There were a lot of nurses in the hospital, but here you're on your own."

"Don't you think I'm qualified to take care of him by myself?"

That wasn't what he'd meant at all. Arden was surprised by the plea for reassurance in Rachel's question. Usually, she seemed so confident. "I can't think of anyone better qualified to

LIEXP0320

take care of him. But he's got a long road to recovery ahead, and you're going to need help so you don't wear yourself out."

"I told Hadassah I'd *wilkom* her help, but I don't think I can count on her. Joyce and Albert won't return from Canada for a couple more weeks, according to Ivan."

"In addition to Grace, there are others in the community who will be *hallich* to help."

"I don't know about that. I'm worried they'll stay away because of my presence. Maybe Ivan would have been better off without me here. Maybe my coming here was a mistake."

"*Neh.* It wasn't a mistake." Upon seeing the fragile vulnerability in Rachel's eyes, Arden's heart ballooned with compassion. "Trust me, the community will *kumme* to help."

"In that case, I'd better keep dessert and tea on hand," Rachel said, smiling once again.

"Does that mean we can't have a slice of that pie over there?"

"Of course it doesn't. And since Ivan has no appetite, you and I might as well have large pieces."

Supping with Rachel after a hard day's work, encouraging her and discussing Ivan's care as if he were…not a child, but *like* a child, felt… Well, it felt like how Arden always imagined it would feel if he had a family of his own. Which was probably why, half an hour later as he directed his horse toward home, Arden's stomach was full, but he couldn't shake the aching emptiness he felt inside.

She is going back, so I'd better not get too accustomed to her company, as pleasant as it's turning out to be.

Don't miss
The Amish Nurse's Suitor *by Carrie Lighte,*
available April 2020 wherever
Love Inspired books and ebooks are sold.

LoveInspired.com